I0722367

SHADELANDS

RACHEL RANDALL

ARGYLE FOX
PUBLISHING

SHADELANDS

CHAPTER 1

Nia groaned at the repetitive, mind-numbing lullaby playing in her head. She couldn't remember where she'd first heard the dark tune and she didn't care, so long as it stopped. Much to her frustration, it didn't. Shifting restlessly while sitting cross-legged on a molding straw mattress, she glared at a broken armchair pushed against a moss-covered wall. The chair looked lifeless and empty, a perfect metaphor for her life.

The song finally concluded. Nia sighed in relief, flicked a flea off her knee, and stood up. *Maybe moving around will keep the tune from replaying,* she thought hopefully.

Maneuvering in the dim light, she tiptoed around piles of rotting garbage on a loudly creaking floor. Cockroaches scattered at her feet. At a barred window overlooking a dark and narrow street lined with ruined cottages like her own, she halted. The lullaby resumed.

"I wonder what time it's supposed to be," she said to the empty room.

To her relief, the song stopped. In its place, a curt inner voice answered, *Work time. Go get the flour from the miller's and bring it to the bakery.*

Thankful the music had ceased, Nia tripped toward the door, accidentally dislodging a pinecone buried in the rubbish. Distracted by the strange object, she stubbed her toe on the threshold. Her inner voice sighed in agitation.

"Small, useless thing," she muttered, kicking the pinecone irritably outside. "Stop getting in my way."

With excessive care, she stepped over the threshold and shut the door behind her. Automatically, her gaze lowered to her bare feet and the coal-dusted stone pathway outside her hut.

"If I keep looking at my feet, maybe I won't bother people this time," Nia whispered. Hot tears sprang to her eyes at the thought.

The air was thicker and harder to breathe than usual. The low, ash-choked light was dim, causing her to stumble painfully over sharp gravel she couldn't see. Not many paces from home, she began coughing and spluttering. A block away, someone else wheezed.

Anxiety flooded Nia's senses. Her palms grew wet with sweat.

Oh no! she thought in terror. *My next-door neighbor. Keep your eyes down!*

Determined to avoid unwanted attention, she held her breath as the woman approached. Old, weathered feet flashed in and out of Nia's view. Despite a sudden welling of loneliness, Nia didn't look up. She didn't greet her neighbor. Her neighbor didn't greet her. Soon the wheezing and coughing faded into the distance.

Her heart pounding within her, Nia fearfully passed several more figures on the way to the mill. She knew them all by their feet and coughs. What they looked like beyond that was anyone's guess.

At last, she reached the base of the mill door. Pausing on the threshold, she stared at the crack beneath the entrance and waited. She never had to knock. Sooner or later, the door would open on its own, revealing the miller's feet. Nia would follow those familiar feet inside, where a bag of flour awaited. This morning, to her surprise, the miller didn't appear.

A rotten, acridly sweet smell wafted to her nostrils. She tried to ignore it, but curiosity got the better of her. Glancing to her right, she gasped. Nia had never seen the bottoms of the miller's feet, but there they were. Flies buzzed around them. Her gaze started to wander up the bloodless legs to the rest of the body lying on the ground, when suddenly, her whole head felt like it had been jolted with electricity. In anguish, she returned her gaze to the base of the door. With the miller dead, would anyone open it for her?

Nia figured the answer was no, and she still needed her flour. Deciding no one else ought to be inconvenienced for her, she pushed against the door. To her relief, it was unlocked. Walking silently toward the back wall, she passed piles of cockroach-infested garbage as she moved toward lines of flour sacks. One bag was half full. It looked like the miller had been filling it but left the job unfinished. Nia's breath caught. *Is this the last sack he touched?* Shoving the thought aside, she tied it for him. *The miller always gives me lighter loads anyway, since I can't carry as much as the adults. What does it matter if it's a little smaller than usual?* she wondered. Shouldering the bag, she headed to the bakery.

Glowing embers on a blackened, cobbled floor greeted Nia when she entered the small, hot building. Ignoring the coals, she dropped her sack next to the kneading bakers. From the corner of her eye she watched them working at the dough troughs, their soot-smeared, leathery faces dripping sweat into the dough they kneaded and punched. It was horrible work. But she didn't pity them. She had a more basic need.

Nia's stomach growled while she waited for her daily ration. Hungry as she was, she didn't dare interrupt the bakers. Their work looked more important than anything she was good for.

Several minutes passed. Still, no one seemed to notice her. Despite her best efforts to quench it, the old loneliness tugged at her. Nia longed for someone to talk to her, even if it meant getting scolded for being a burden. As she stared at the dying embers on the bakery floor, she felt her courage gather. But upon opening her mouth to speak up, a worker's feet approached her. A moment later, an exceedingly small, round cake of soot-blackened flatbread rested in her hands. Astounded at its meagerness, Nia didn't thank him. The worker didn't seem to care.

Walking out of the bakery with a heavy heart, she heard the voice say clearly, *Go to the well and quench your thirst. Better to not have you lying on the ground with flies buzzing all around you.*

"Come to think of it, I'd almost prefer it," Nia whispered darkly to herself.

Two others were at the well when she reached it. Nothing about the day was going smoothly, pushing her anxiety to its peak. Leaning silently against a wall, Nia waited for the others to finish. She imagined their disgust at her presence. After all, no one liked to hurry for a useless girl.

At last, the people finished drawing their water. She started moving forward for hers, when two more arrived, cutting her off. Feeling panic rising, she apologized and hurried away. If she needed water later, she'd go when no one was around.

A few minutes later, Nia was almost home. She didn't remember walking there. Her mind was too distracted. Suddenly, a light materialized on the soot-covered ground around her. Sandaled, glowing feet appeared. Nia stopped cold. She felt as if she'd been slapped, her mind forced back into focus. No one in Shades wore shoes. No one glowed either. Despite her fear of bothering this stranger, she cautiously looked up.

Instantly, her jaw dropped in astonishment. The creature belonging to these feet was a boy—a brilliantly shining boy who was immaculately clean. No hole could be seen in his colorful tunic, pants, or sandals. No grime was smeared onto them. His face was beautiful—achingly so. He wasn't thin and gnarled like most of the townspeople. Rather, he was sturdily built with a nice, straight back. His eyes, though not as bright as his face, resembled the smoldering embers on the bakery floor. Life flickered in them. *Too much life*, Nia thought, shuddering.

A scream caught in her throat. She started to back away, but the boy grabbed her arm and pulled her from the path toward the forest on the edge of town.

"Stop!" Nia cried. "Where are you taking me?" As she finished the question, her shoulder felt lighter somehow, as if part of her was missing.

"I'm taking you out of here, you poor thing! When was the last time you had a bath?" the glowing boy replied, holding his nose. "Good," he said, his face breaking into a grin, "looks like I knocked the imp off of you."

"Imp?" Nia asked. "What in Shades is that? Who are you? Let go! You're hurting me!"

The boy complied.

"I'm sorry," he said. "It's just that I'm in a bit of a hurry. I told myself I'd save someone from the Shadelands, and that's what I'm trying to do. My name's Tanni, by the way. I'm a Starbeam from a township near Sunburst, and well, I'm here to rescue you."

"Rescue me?" gasped Nia, feeling the missing part of her return. "Rescue me from what?"

"From that!" Tanni exclaimed, pointing at Nia and backing away from her. "The thing on your shoulder. Can't you see him? It's an imp about a foot tall, and he's growling at me like a vicious dog."

Nia looked at her shoulder and saw nothing. She brushed it off for good measure.

"An imp?" she asked. "What do you mean?"

"Never mind," Tanni said, his smile fading. "From your hesitation it's clear you won't be coming with me."

"Why not?" Nia wondered, tilting her head at him

"That thing appears to have too great a hold on you."

"What thing?"

"The imp," Tanni sighed and inched closer to the forest. "Listen, I'll give you one last chance to follow me. I could try to knock the imp off you again later, but not here. Not with so many more imps on the prowl."

"I'd follow you, if I had an idea of where you were going," Nia muttered, shocked to hear the words come out of her mouth.

"To Sunburst, the City of Light," said Tanni.

Nia was baffled. She'd never heard of Sunburst before.

Noticing her confusion, Tanni explained, "Sunburst is the home of all true Starbeams. Trust me, you'd love it there. It's so beautiful. The place positively glows."

With that, Tanni's smile returned. Nia was intrigued. Her eyes flickered with interest.

"By the way," Tanni said, "what is your name?"

Nia thought for a long moment, trying to remember the answer. At last, she said tentatively, "Um, I think it's Nia."

"You're Nia?" Tanni moved toward her. He seemed to glow brighter. "Wait, are you Tessa and Tomi's daughter?"

Nia's heart skipped. "How do you know my parents?" she demanded, her cheeks flushing at the memories flooding her mind.

"They've been looking for you for like, forever! I can't believe I'm the one who actually found you! Come, Nia," Tanni said, reaching his hand toward her. "Come home. They want to see you so badly. I promise, you won't receive another offer like this again."

Nia considered the offer and stretched her hand out to his. Just as their hands were about to meet, the song returned. It was painfully loud, and terribly mind numbing. The voice hissed throughout the tune, *Nonsense! Can't you see how dangerous this boy is? He was pulling you into the woods a moment ago to kill you. No one would have heard you scream. So what if he knows who your parents are? Most killers do! Never trust a person who glows. It's the sign of a murderer!*

Nia turned stark white and jerked her hand from Tanni's reach.

She backed away from him, her face riddled with fear. Tanni moved toward her, confused.

"Stop! Stay away from me," Nia shuddered, her gaze lowering to Tanni's feet. "You're just luring me away to kill me!"

"Kill you?" Tanni cried. "Nonsense! The imp's manipulating you. Can't you see?"

But it was no use. Nia turned and fled. She wouldn't see him again for many days.

CHAPTER 2

That night, Nia slept fitfully. Meanwhile, on a ruined dresser nearby, a small, gargoyle-like creature brooded over Tanni. His name was Pester, and he was greatly annoyed.

"The insolent Starbeam nearly took you away from me, the only sign I'm worth anything. Unlike Lord Accuse, I can't get away without a drudge. You're my food source," he muttered bitterly. "Before today, I thought you were under my control. But the illusion is shattered. Curse that boy!"

Pester reflected on his next moves. Scratching his chin and picking at his teeth, he said dully, "Making you depressed again takes so much work. Even worse, it depresses me. I'm not one to challenge conventional wisdom, but did the Originals really have to set it up this way? Was there really no other option? Ugh! If Vex ever found out the sorts of things I whisper in the dark . . ."

A scratch at the cottage door made Pester jump.

"Who's there?" he demanded.

"It's Addle," replied a gravelly imp voice. "Vex wants a town meeting."

"Now?" Pester peered at Nia and wondered how much longer she would sleep. If she awakened with him gone, his plan would be that much more difficult to carry out.

"Yes, now," said Addle testily.

Pester slammed a fist on the dresser. Despite the noise, Nia continued sleeping. Frustrated, he flew through a trapdoor in the rafters. Outside, he was greeted by Addle's grimace. Beside Addle were Pester's two sisters, Wither and Taunt. They scowled at him.

"We tried to get Vex to leave you out of this, but he insisted on you joining us. Happy?" Wither huffed. "Ugh, I can hardly look at you! Our drudges have been restless since Nia ran into them at the well and apologized to their faces. To their faces!"

"You should have sensed their confusion," Taunt snarled. "They almost woke up because of your idiotic recklessness. What in Shades were you thinking by bringing her there at that hour? I thought we had an agreement. Nia goes to the well around ten. We go there half past nine. Did you forget?"

Pester bristled. Wagging an angry finger at his sisters, he cried, "It wasn't my fault! With the miller dead, Nia carried a flour sack less than half the amount of its usual weight. It took her less time because of it. It couldn't be helped, and it couldn't be expected!"

"Can you three love birds pipe down?" Addle wrung his hands. "Vex is waiting for us on the other end of town."

Taunt growled, and Wither breathed heavily. Pester rolled his eyes. That was answer enough for Addle. He leapt in the air, and the four of them took to the skies. Below, soot-covered shacks passed by, one after another. As they flew, Pester came alongside Addle.

"Who else is coming?" he asked.

"Just about everyone," Addle said, whisking past a smoking chimney. "I was tasked to get your family and you. Daze had the large Heckle clan, and Bore was given Stupor and his many kin."

Pester's eyes narrowed, "Is this about the sprite that came into town sitting on the Starbeam's shoulder?" The dainty creature had kept him from attacking Tanni earlier. She was two or three inches smaller than Pester, but he knew to keep his distance. Sprites could turn an incautious imp into dust in a matter of seconds.

Addle gave a curt nod and spat.

"Is the sprite really dangerous enough to need everybody in the village?" Pester wondered.

Addle wiped the spittle from his lips and gave Pester a sober look. "We're taking no chances," he began. "With the whole group of us, Vex claims the sprite might give up without a fight. We can't afford to lose anyone. Whether some of us like it or not, we depend on each other to keep the town running smoothly." As he said this, Addle eyed Wither and Taunt, who scowled in return.

When they arrived, the town hall roof crawled with imps. Pester estimated there were at least a hundred of them. Implings, or those under a year of age, were wisely excluded. Pester was just looking for a place to land, when Vex approached. The large imp bared his teeth.

"You're the last one here," he said icily. "Took long enough."

Pester alighted on a vacant spot. Looking away from Vex, he peered in amazement at so many imps gathered in one place.

"Blame Addle and my sisters," Pester at last said stiffly. "I only found out about this five minutes ago."

Vex settled next to him and glared at the side of Pester's face until he turned to look at him.

"Is that so?" Vex sneered. "Your sisters showed up here without you, claiming you refused the invitation. Addle said that was news to him, so I sent the three of them back for you. You're lucky Taunt and Wither were lying. It wouldn't have boded well for you if they'd spoken truthfully."

Pester stared calmly into Vex's cold, black gaze. Trying to appear unruffled, he stretched his arms and yawned, "Well, I'm here, aren't I? Anyone who knows my sisters knows they can't speak a true word about me. I wouldn't be surprised if they claimed I was on the sprite's side."

Vex smirked. Pester wasn't far off the mark.

"Why, those good for nothing, spiteful, double crossing—"

"Sisters are sisters," Vex said impatiently. "Let's get started."

With that, Vex flew to the top of a podium in the center of the gathering, landed, and called for order. His booming voice caused everyone gathered on the roof to snap to attention. "First off, is there any idiot still clueless why I called for this meeting tonight? No? Good.

"Citizens of Shades," Vex continued, "a deadly sprite lurks somewhere nearby, waiting to strike. She knows our defenses and the layout of the town, having passed through this morning unchallenged by anyone, riding on the shoulder of a fully glowing Starbeam. Who was supposed to be on guard duty? I want names." Vex paused and scanned the gathering. His look was met with determined silence. "Fine," he scowled. "Don't speak up. I'll find out one way or another."

The crowd shifted nervously. Making sure Vex wasn't looking at him, Pester rolled his eyes.

"We all know what havoc a sprite can wreak, don't we, Heckle?" Vex asked, meeting the battle-scarred imp's one remaining eye. Heckle shifted uneasily and hid his missing hand. Vex stared at him in somber silence before turning back to the crowd. "I want no casualties like Heckle's tonight. In other words," he said grimly, "don't shed blood if the sprite is willing to surrender. The sprite's agony watching her Starbeam become a drudge is the type of torture I don't want to miss.

"Everyone pair up. Find someone trustworthy. I'm pairing with Pester. Everyone else find your partner, then stop talking. Got it?"

Pester blinked. Vex was an Original, or one of the first imps to arrive in the Shadelands. He called Pester a useless underling. Pester was pretty sure the ancient imp hated him. Why would Vex choose him for his partner?

A din of voices filled the air, as the crowd of imps called for partners. Vex remained stiffly at his post, shooting dark looks Pester's way. As the rooftop became silent once more, Pester felt a chill go down his back.

"Everyone paired up?" asked Vex, his glittering eyes surveying the crowd. "Good. The sprite and her Starbeam are two miles due east in the Wanderer's Forest. Go silently. Contain the sprite first. Don't wake the boy. I don't want him slipping away."

"Do we use spells?" Bore called out from deep within the crowd.

"Yes, Bore. Preferably a killing spell on yourself," Vex shook his head irritably. "Magic's fine. Just try not to blow yourself up. Everyone else ready? Move out."

Vex joined Pester on the eastern side of the roof and the two of them took flight. Pester remained puzzled. Why was Vex gliding beside him?

The sizable group flew silently behind Pester and Vex. A deadly purpose glinted in each beady eye. They sliced through the air like phantoms, skimming the coal-dusted treetops of the Wanderer's Forest as they searched for the sprite and Starbeam.

A few minutes into the hunt, a lit-up circle of canopy came into view. Vex quietly ordered the imp pairs into attack positions, then turned to Pester.

"What?" Pester mouthed.

Vex motioned to a nearby treetop. No sooner had Pester landed there beside him, when Vex whispered tensely, "Grab the sprite when she surrenders."

"What?" Pester gasped.

"Don't hurt her. Don't panic and blow her up if she injures you. Keep a steady head," Vex commanded. "I'll be behind you to take her once she's contained."

"Do I have a choice in this?" Pester asked through gritted teeth.

"No," said Vex, his tone dangerous.

Now, Pester understood why Vex chose him for a partner. Of all the imps in Shades, he was the most expendable. "Curse you," he muttered darkly.

"Enough!" Vex stepped menacingly toward him. "Catch that sprite!"

Pester scowled and gave a curt nod. It was just like Vex to sacrifice an underling to save his own skin. Pester's heart hammered as he descended with the troupe through the canopy. As he approached the ground, the sleeping boy and his sprite came into view. *If the sprite remains unaware of us, perhaps I can capture her without a struggle.* His heart lightened at the thought.

Suddenly, the sprite turned her head and made direct eye contact with Pester. He nearly fell from the sky in fright.

"Intruders!" the sprite shrieked. "Tanni, wake up, wake up!" She slapped the Starbeam's cheek with her tiny hand, but the boy didn't stir. Taking to the air, the sprite dashed left and right, a wall of imps awaiting her at every turn. She screamed again and again for Tanni, but still he slept.

To Pester's bemusement, Bore and his partner were the first fools to close in. They almost reached attacking distance when the sprite flashed a blinding light at them. The light was so bright Pester thought a lightning bolt had struck the trees. In horror, he watched the two unlucky imps transform into a small dust cloud that floated softly to the ground.

The war screams stopped. In its place was an eerie silence.

Pester clung feebly to the canopy, paralyzed. In his mind's eye, he relived the moment his mother, too, vanished in a puff of dust. Reeling from the trauma, he hardly noticed a floodgate of spells breaking out from every quadrant. A spell whizzed by his ear, snapping him out of his momentary trance. Quickly, he cast a shield on himself. It wouldn't block the sprite's lightening, but it would protect him from friendly fire.

SHADELANDS

The air crackled with volleys cast by furious imps. Somehow the sprite dodged all of them. Imps without shields weren't so lucky. Their screeches, moans, and groans filled the air as they were struck by friendly fire. Chaos ensued. Out of the corner of his eye, Pester noticed Vex. The oversized imp watched the battle coolly. When Heckle passed in front him, Vex grabbed the one-handed imp.

"Cast a sleeping spell on the boy before he wakes up and runs!" he commanded.

Heckle obeyed.

The battle intensified. Flashes of light exploded from the sprite's body, killing half a dozen imps at once. Several imps crashed to the ground and lay still. Others screamed they could no longer see. One blinded imp crashed into Pester before clawing helplessly at a nearby tree.

As Pester wondered if the blinded imp could have his sight restored, one of the sprite's flashes surged toward him. This one was coming too fast. It would hit him head on. Squeezing his eyes shut, he braced for impact. *I'm going to die*, he thought in terror. His whole body went tense, awaiting death. But it didn't come. Instead, the searing heat wrapped around him and gradually dissipated. Opening his eyes, he found himself the only unharmed imp within the blast radius. He couldn't believe his luck. Shaken, he flew out of dodge and landed on a protected branch. A wave of guilt overcame him. He shouldn't have survived.

For two minutes, Pester reeled while the battle raged on without him. Then, a spell struck the sprite's arm. Instantly, her arm fell to her side. Desperate, she continued throwing light enchantments. But with her good arm rendered useless and her magic store nearly spent, her light became weak. Panting and trembling, she backed against a tree and raised her remaining arm as pitiful protection shield against the imps' raining spells.

Diving through the canopy, Pester flung a shielding spell

between the sprite and the continuing onslaught. All around him, imps bewitched with confusion magic fought each other. But those who'd been smart enough to shield themselves from friendly fire joined in behind Pester.

The sprite's eyes were wide with horror. Tears glistened on her cheek. Though he believed her a monster, Pester was filled with pity. "Surrender now, and no more harm will come to you," he said coldly.

"Some promise coming from an imp," she said. A tear dripped from her chin.

"Would you rather I kill you?" Pester sneered.

The sprite locked eyes with him. Despite the tears, there was no fear present in her gaze. He was taken aback. "Yes," she said firmly.

Swallowing his admiration, Pester cast a sleeping spell on the sprite and caught her limp body as she collapsed. Her body was warm and smelled like fresh air. Taking in her lovely features, he was horrified. *She's a murderer. Just a murderer*, he thought. His heart told him otherwise. Killing others wasn't her intention. If she'd wanted to inflict real harm, she could have torn through the town and wiped everyone out. No, this wasn't a killer. This was a frightened creature who'd defended herself and the Starbeam child she loved.

What have I done? Pester wondered in remorse. *I'm delivering her to be tortured by a real monster. Does she deserve this?*

Vex cleared his throat behind him. Pester turned and swallowed down his emotion.

"I have her," he said gruffly. "You can capture the Starbeam now."

CHAPTER 3

Loneliness consumed Nia. Pulling her hair in frustration, she wanted to scream, but her throat hurt too much. It was Tanni's fault. His presence reminded her how she'd ended up here in the first place. She sat on her mattress and stared at the cobwebbed ceiling, reliving her mother's farewell to her over and over.

Nia was only five years old when her mother went into labor. As a favor to Nia's parents, Nanna came and took her to her cottage to stay for a bit. Everything was fun for the first three days. Then, Nanna caught a fever from Nia. The sickness made her grumpy. Nia tried staying out of her way with little success. Though feverish, Nanna still had to tend to the fire. While dragging herself across the room one morning, she stepped on one of Nia's wooden blocks, sending her stumbling against a couch.

"Must you burden me so?" she screamed at her granddaughter. "Must you be such a nuisance? What were you thinking?"

"Oh Nanna, I'm so sorry!" Nia said, starting to cry. "I'll play outside. I'll try not to burden you anymore." She tore out of the house. Nanna called after her, but she kept running, seeking a safe place to hide. She got her wish. As she ran, a strange forest manifested around her, followed by empty blackness.

Nia shivered. The flashback still hurt. Her Nanna's words still cut. She hated herself for being a nuisance to her grandmother. She regretted everything and stared out the dark window, willing her mind to go blank.

The blankness didn't come. Instead, the memory of Tanni's light penetrated her consciousness. Gasping, Nia saw Tanni's burning eyes stare directly into hers. Who was this boy? He certainly wasn't a murderer. The idea now sounded preposterous – absurd. *Why in stars did I ever think that?* she wondered. *Did that thought come from the invisible imp the Starbeam claimed sits on my shoulder?*

"If so," Nia said out loud, her voice scratchy, her throat burning, "why can't I see him?"

It was two days since she met the Starbeam. She hadn't been outside since. Yesterday, she was too depressed to get up, and now, feeling under the weather, she had no desire to get up, despite the voice urging her to visit the miller. Just the thought of it made her head swim. *No miller, no bakery. No bakery, no bread*, the voice reminded her. *Aren't you hungry?*

No, she wasn't hungry. Nia ran her tongue around the inside of dry lips. She needed water. Carefully, she pushed herself to her feet. For a moment, everything went black and she nearly swooned. As sight restored, the room spun around her. Gathering her senses, she maneuvered around piles of garbage and headed blearily toward the door. She pushed it open. As if on cue, the song started again. Its effect wasn't as strong as usual, but it set her head pounding.

Just outside her hut, Nia stopped and arched her back. Her whole body ached in protest. A wave of nausea came over her. Quickly finishing her stretch, she stared at the soot-choked sky. *Has it always been this dark?* she wondered. Suddenly dizzy again, she caught herself against the threshold. The spinning stopped long enough for her to move again. She swayed unsteadily toward the well.

SHADELANDS

The lullaby faltered mid-phrase before starting again in earnest. Nia tried shutting it out, but the tune continued incessantly. For the first time, she realized Tanni might be right. That devilish song might just be the work of an imp. Each time she refocused her mind on anything besides the song, the tune redoubled its efforts, until everything was scattered and disjointed in her head. Nevertheless, she kept her head up; a choice she soon regretted.

Stranger after stranger passed along the path. Nia looked each of them in the face, her anxiety growing to a crescendo. Eventually, she couldn't stand it any longer. Dropping her gaze to the strangers' feet, she gasped. She knew these strangers. Astounded, she looked again at the unfamiliar faces. Her next-door neighbor with old and weathered feet had an old and weathered face to match. Her brow was riddled with deep care lines and had an expression of hopelessness. A man missing two toes on his left foot also had a missing nose. He too appeared entirely hopeless. So did every other person in town. Despite the song, Nia wondered what she'd looked like to Tanni. Why did he single out someone who was so obviously useless?

At the well, she joined a line of disheartened, shattered people, blankly awaiting their turn for a drink of filthy water. Their features swam in Nia's vision until, her eyes clouded by fever, she saw her parents in the faces of these pitiful strangers.

Nia knew her parents had been beautiful, especially her mother, whose infectious smile used to set her giggling. But the people in the vision before her had little beauty left to them. They were like two rocks broken and weathered by countless storms. She choked back a cry. Dry heaves seized her. Between sobs and wretches, she called out weakly for her mother. Neither person looked up at her. They simply clung to their water pitchers, unaware of her turmoil.

The lullaby reached a fever pitch. Between the numbing verses, Nia continued to call to the people she imagined were her parents. Their faces twisted grotesquely with fear. Then, they turned and fled without a backward glance, their jugs sloshing as they went.

Nausea and dizziness overwhelmed Nia. She faced away from the well and vomited into the dirt. A cold, clammy sweat set her shivering. Her vision swam.

Get some water quick. Then head home before you faint, the voice said sternly.

"But my parents," Nia murmured. "My parents."

What? You thought you saw your parents? No. You're hallucinating. Your fevered brain is flashing images at you. Now get your drink before you die of dehydration!

Nia vomited again where she stood in line, shivering uncontrollably. Someone handed her a clay pitcher filled with the well's cloudy water. *There,* the voice said. *You have your drink. Get home before you pass out on the path.* Clutching the vessel, she stumbled toward her cottage.

The hallucinations began with the first step. Suddenly, her parents were in front of her again. This time they smiled at her with eerie grins before backing away at astonishing speed.

"Mom, Dad, don't go!" Nia reached feebly for her parents. Farther down the path, they again appeared, wearing the same unsettling smiles, and gliding away backward once more. Nia was crying now. The tears splashed into her water pitcher. "Stop running from me! It's your daughter, Nia. Come back! Why don't you want me anymore?"

Wow, that vision just keeps repeating for you. You know it's not real, right? the voice said. She nodded and stopped. Again, she felt she was going to be sick.

Somehow, Nia made it back inside her cottage. Setting the pitcher on the splintered bedside table, she looked up. Her parents looked back at her from the ceiling with twisted grins and sunken, dark eyes. Almost ludicrous with fever, she whimpered to them to get off the ceiling and help her. They didn't move.

"It's because I'm a burden, isn't it? It's because you didn't need me anymore, right? I'm sorry I grew up. I'm sorry I didn't stay a baby. Is that why you decided to have another one and send me off with Nanna?" Nia choked. The sweat that was beading on her forehead began dribbling into her eyes.

The room was spinning again. She lay down and clutched the sides of her bed to steady herself.

See? the voice cried. *That meeting with the intruder the other day nearly did you in. Hope you've learned your lesson. Strangers carry nothing but diseases. Try avoiding them from now on.* Nia listened to the only coherent words in a world of broken thoughts. But the fever was too much. Even those words didn't make sense for long.

CHAPTER 4

Nia's fever spiked and reached dangerous heights. Pester was used to the child suffering an occasional cold or light sickness, but this was something else. The intensity blindsided the imp. Granted, he was relieved to have Nia's mind quiet and miserable without his intervention, but the hallucinations left him alarmed. The girl was delirious. Every half hour or so, dry heaves wracked her fragile, skeletal frame. In the minutes between heaves, she shivered uncontrollably. Weak and incoherent, she cried out continuously for her parents, reaching out toward the oddest of locations as if they were there. Her voice was parched and scratchy, reminding Pester of crackling, dead leaves. Soon, she lost it altogether.

The imp was unnerved. Nia's cries reminded him of his mother's feeble voice calling out for his father. Yet, Pester's father wasn't an Original. He couldn't have stopped what happened next. He couldn't have stopped his mate from disintegrating. Pester flinched at the scene seared into his memory. Would he watch Nia die too? Did he care if she did?

During the first day of fever, Pester often urged Nia to drink from the clay pitcher. But it only led to more vomiting. Soon, the girl refused to drink. Nevertheless, he shrugged this off, assuming a night of rest would help. However, as dim light filtered through the ash-clogged sky on the second day, Nia grew worse. Turning her head weakly from side to side, she let out a low moan, her fever-crusted eyes sealed shut. Her olive-toned skin was pale and had a yellowish tint. The girl's lips were parched and cracked. "Mamma," she muttered repeatedly. "Mamma . . . Mamma . . ." Despite his instincts, Pester grew to pity his drudge. Listening to her was almost unbearable.

"Child, get up," he urged her. "Drink something."

Nia was unresponsive. Pester leapt onto the ruined mattress above her black, matted hair. He reached out a tentative hand and felt her forehead, which burned to the touch. Closing his eyes, he peered within her body, hoping to find that Nia had the proper immune response to fight this sickness. He found nothing. She was slowly dying. Pester let out a hiss, then flew into the rafters, where he deliberated for several minutes.

No one would blame him for abandoning his drudge. It was almost expected that imps with weak Starbeams should help death along so they could move on to a better one. The temptation almost overpowered him. The energy he gleaned from her was pitiful. He didn't have the same inroads with her as other imps with their drudges. Without his drudge's energy, he didn't have magic. Without magic, he was nothing.

"Well, she's almost dead," Pester muttered in a voice that was low and dark. "What have I to do with a dying skeleton? If only she were dead already."

As soon as he said this, an icy chill shot through his heart. Sucking in a breath, he stared at Nia with eyes wide as saucers. He wouldn't abandon her—couldn't abandon her. His own foolish words bound him to her. The memory burned him to the core. "I swore an oath," he cried, tearing furiously at the few wispy hairs on his bald head. "I swore it to her face! What an idiot I am! But I didn't know then. I just wanted the stubborn waif to trust me."

For hours Pester wrestled with himself, seeking a way to end Nia's life without breaking his oath. But he found none. Meanwhile, Nia continued to deteriorate.

Around midnight, an alarming realization crept into his mind. It struck him hard, so hard it nearly caused him to fall off the rafter. If he refused Nia any interventions and watched her die, he'd become an oath breaker. Of all the things Pester was and could become, this was worst of all.

Oath breakers lost huge portions of their magic. Spells acquired over a lifetime became lost forever. It would be devastating. The mental anguish would be even worse. No imp from the mines could live with such a damaging title. Their pride wouldn't allow it.

Reeling from this revelation, Pester shrieked and leaped to the trapdoor on the ceiling. He flew into the polluted night sky, racing toward the only imp he knew in Shades who remembered how to cast healing runes.

Vex was once a sprite. As part of the generation that rebelled and was chased out of the Sunlands alongside the imp lord, Accuse, Vex still retained some sprite magic. Everyone knew because he bragged about it constantly. Yet, Pester also knew coaxing out an actual sprite spell—a healing rune, no less—would be challenging. But he had to try. There was no other option.

Alighting on Vex's roof, Pester rapped on the trapdoor. "Oy Vex, you in there?"

After a slight pause, Vex yelled back rather testily, "That you, Pester? I'm busy conquering a new drudge."

"Yeah, I'm aware of that. But this is important," Pester cried, sucking in a deep breath. "I need you to teach me how to cast a healing spell." He grimaced. The request was ridiculous, and he knew it as soon as it came out of his mouth.

Vex was incredulous. "You what?" He opened the hatch and stared at the young imp. At last he sneered, "Trying to become a sprite, Pester? Imp lands getting a little too boring?"

"Of course not!" Pester said, bristling. "You know how I hate sprites. Listen, Nia's deathly ill. It's quite possible she's dying."

Vex shrugged, "So?"

"Look," Pester said, "I know your drudge caused it. I mean, I can hear him retching inside the hut from here. So, all I'm asking in recompense is that you teach me a little healing spell to make up for the damage he inflicted. Once I know it, I'll stop bothering you."

"You're mistaken if you think I owe you anything. I'm in no way, shape, or form responsible if your drudge dies," Vex said coldly. "Besides, if you didn't want her dying of a foreign illness, you should've been more responsible. You should have steered her clear of the boy before they made first contact. What a waste of my time."

Vex turned to leave. In desperation Pester grabbed the hatch. "But just a month ago you showed Addle, didn't you?"

"Yes, for Addle's drudge, but he wasn't allowed to cast it himself," Vex hissed, glaring at Pester's hand, which held fast to his door. "I did that in return for a favor, of which I owe you none. Besides, you're not an Original like myself. You'd blow yourself up along with the rest of your neighbors just in the casting attempt. Only sprites and former sprites can handle it." His eyes met Pester's. "Let Nia die. You and everyone in Shades would be better off for it. Goodbye."

Pester's hand fell limp to his side as Vex closed the hatch door behind himself. Helpless, only one thought consoled him. He wouldn't be considered an oath breaker. After all, he tried everything he could. With a lightened heart, he started toward his home. Passing by the mill warehouse, a dim light inside caught his eye. Pester scowled. That was where Vex had imprisoned the sprite.

Pester stopped in mid-air. A new thought flooded over him, sickening him to the core. He wasn't in the clear yet.

This is not happening, he thought angrily, darting to the mill. He threw open the small imp door above the large one used by drudges and flew inside. Scanning the rafters, he spotted the sprite, triple bound with holding spells, lying listlessly in the back corner. Racing to her incautiously, Pester grabbed her shoulders. Just as he was about to shake her awake, the sprite lit up with a brilliant burst of light, slamming him against a rafter post. His insides felt like they were being fried. The pain was so intense, he couldn't breathe. The light lasted only a moment, but it felt an eternity. When it stopped, Pester slumped against the rafter beam. Feeling half cooked with the wind knocked out of him, he realized he couldn't lay down. Somehow, the sprite's burst bound him to the post.

He began straining against the invisible binding, when the sprite, whom he assumed was asleep, lifted her head.

"Odd," she said softly, "that blast should have killed you. At the least, you should have slowly crumbled to dust by this point. Perhaps if I tried it again?"

"No, don't! I come in peace!" Pester wheezed through burning lungs. Cowering feebly, he felt vulnerable and weak.

"Peace?" asked the sprite. Her fiery gaze made him squirm. "What do you know of peace?"

"Very little, I'll admit. But I swear I didn't come here looking for trouble," Pester whimpered, his heart pounding. His skin smarted and steamed. The sight terrified him. *What is this strange magic?* In desperation, he looked at the sprite. "What's that word the drudges cry when they're being captured? Mercy, I believe it is. Yes, mercy!"

The sprite scrutinized Pester for a long moment. Then, Pester's bonds loosened and disappeared. Though seemingly free, he was drawn toward her, until he stood before her rooted to the spot as her prisoner. The sprite glared at Pester. "You were the one I asked to kill me so I wouldn't be taken prisoner, and you cast sleep on me instead. What have you to say for yourself?"

Pester trembled and choked on his words, "If—if I'd killed you, Vex would have killed me. I was under orders, I swear!"

"I see. You were his unwitting pawn. I forgive you now." The air lightened, and the burning of Pester's skin and insides eased. "Tell me, peaceful one, why are you here? I doubt it was for the purpose of gloating over me. You don't seem the stupid type."

Traumatized from nearly being fried to dust, Pester had forgotten why he'd come. Panting, he stammered, but no coherent answer came out.

The sprite chuckled, "Perhaps if you were a little calmer? Would that help?"

As the words escaped the sprite's mouth, peace washed over him. His shaking ceased. "How do you do that?" Pester asked incredulously. "You're bound hand and foot to a rafter. You can barely move. How are you casting magic without moving?"

"My light can move for me. Since my capture, I've had time to recharge it. Now will you tell me why you're here?"

"It's my drudge," he blurted. "She's dying. I think your Starbeam made her sick, so this mess is entirely your fault. You owe me—so, so teach me how to heal her."

"Are you mad? You'd blow yourself up!" the sprite exclaimed. "Besides, what do you care if she dies? Imps care nothing for the health of their Starbeams. Why should you?"

"I don't! I couldn't care less how healthy she is. It's just that I promised her . . ." *Curses!* he thought. *If only I'd kept my mouth shut!*

"You made a promise to her?" The sprite raised an eyebrow in disbelief.

"I promised to take care of her as a father would his favored child," Pester said bitterly.

The sprite gasped. Again, she scrutinized Pester from head to toe. Blowing out a long, hard breath, she formed her mouth into a tight line, and scraped a clawed finger across the rafter she was bound to. The scraping continued and then stopped. Crumpling over, she lay there breathing hard. Pester realized he was no longer held under her spell.

"There," she said, her voice strained from working against her bonds. "Study this rune carefully. It's the easiest one I could give you. It shouldn't deplete all your magic reserves either. That said, don't mess it up, or you really will blow yourself up."

Pester looked behind the sprite's back and studied the rune she'd carved there for him. "This will cure my drudge?"

"Yes, but slowly," said the sprite. Her breathing was coming easier now, but her exhaustion remained. "The rune will trigger the immune response your Starbeam lacks and keep her from dehydrating. You can expect her to fully recover in the next couple days."

Something warmed inside Pester. It was a foreign experience, and he suspected it was due to what just happened. He'd been shown a favor by a sprite. Nodding curtly at the temporarily weak creature, he turned and flew off for his home.

"Farewell," the sprite said. But Pester didn't hear her. He was already halfway home.

Once inside the cottage, Pester hovered over Nia and landed softly above her matted hair. Her forehead was damp with sweat. Steadying his trembling hand and bracing for an explosion, he timidly drew the healing rune on Nia forehead. Instantly, he felt his whole body go weak as the room flashed with a blinding light.

Oh no! I've overdone it, just like my mother! Pester thought in terror. As he fell unconscious, he heard a surprising sound: Nia's breathing grew deeper and more rhythmic. He didn't wake again for two whole days.

CHAPTER 5

Nia's eyes opened slowly. Her nausea was gone, her vision clear. Bracing herself in case the room started spinning again, she looked around nervously. No phantom images met her gaze. The walls and ceiling remained stationary. Seeing this, she sighed in relief, reached for the clay pitcher, and sat up. After a long and gratifying drink, she searched her limited memory for what caused her sickness. Someone had spoken with her. That was all her weakened brain could recall. But who would talk to her? No one in Shades ever did, especially since she avoided conversation.

Nia set her feet on the floor. Her skin felt inflamed and itchy. Tiny red bumps covered her arms and legs. Looking behind her, she recoiled to see her mattress jumping with fleas. Springing to her feet to bat and shake out her tattered tunic, she grimaced as several more fleas tumbled to the floor. She shuddered as they jumped away.

Stepping over to her armchair, Nia feebly leaned her thin, frail frame on it, only to have it crumple beneath her, spilling cockroaches in every direction. Screeching in disgust, she tripped over a garbage pile, and fell to the rotten floor. Sprawled out awkwardly, she focused on a pinecone just in front of her face.

Based on its dull, frayed edges, it had been in her room a long time. Nia closed a fist around it, then, getting back to her feet, she hobbled her way to the door. Panting, she awaited instruction from the voice. Silence. She hummed the hated tune, hoping it would awaken the voice. More silence.

What if the sickness destroyed my ability to think? Nia trembled. After a pause, she decided the only possible course of action would be to follow the voice's previous directions.

"To the miller with you," She recalled, "then to the bakery."

A greasy film coated the door. Nia shuddered as she pushed against it. The door opened to the outside world, where a blackish fog greeted her. Briefly, the memory of a brilliant blue sky over a field of wildflowers sprang to her mind. The contrast between it and this present darkness filled her with unshakable misery. "I live here," she moaned, as she tossed the old pinecone through the dingy fog and out of sight.

Stepping dismally into the fearful, dirty cloud, her lungs burned. After each painful cough, answering coughs came from figures shrouded in the fog. "Who lives like this?" she asked while navigating the well-worn, blackened path to the miller's warehouse.

Acidic dust lodged in the cracks in Nia's bare feet, causing a constant stinging. On either side of the road, the frowning facades of ruined cottages loomed in the fog. Some looked too unsteady to house anyone. Occasionally, a bone lay next to these structures, some wrapped in the remnants of tattered clothing. Her hand went to her mouth, and she fought back tears. Those bones had to belong to dead Shadians. The deceased miller's feet flashed into her memory. One of those bones could be his. Her knees weakened at the thought, and she felt faint.

Shadowy forms drifted in and out of the fog, their gazes vacant. Steering clear of their path, Nia sensed something dark and sinister on each of their shoulders. She darted her gaze toward her own shoulders and was relieved to find nothing. Despite this, she was unsettled and agitated. An overpowering sense of dread overcame her, freezing her in her tracks. She searched her mind for the comforting voice to guide her and met still more silence.

Very well, Nia thought. *If the voice won't tell me where to go, I will.* "Keep going to the miller's," she commanded herself. With a deep breath, she squared her shoulders and walked on, ready to regain some sense of normalcy.

At last, the warehouse mill came into view. Nia approached the door. To her relief, the dead miller had been removed. She stood still. Following the voice's previous instructions, she waited for someone to answer the door. Just as she was ready to walk away, the door swung open.

On the threshold was a mountain of a man, built like chiseled stone. Ragged black hair fell onto his filthy brown shoulders. His only clothes were pants that were shredded just below the knees. Beneath the rags, it was obvious that one of his legs was crooked, as if it had been broken at some point and set incorrectly. Nia sensed a dark presence on his bare left shoulder. She didn't know whether to scream or run. She did neither. Instead, she mutely followed the man when he wordlessly walked back inside.

Within the warehouse, workers sorted through dead cockroaches and ground them into flour. *Wait, I've been eating cockroaches this whole time?* Nia wondered in disgust. *I think I'm going to be sick.*

The man stopped at an enormous sack at the back of the mill. Nia couldn't believe her eyes. She barely had strength left to walk, let alone drag so much flour to the bakery. But she had no choice. If she didn't take the flour, she wouldn't eat. Then, she would join the bones scattered around town.

Gritting her teeth, she reached for the sack. As she did so, mocking laughter echoed in her mind. She froze. The room filled with loud, boisterous chatter. She scanned the warehouse, looking fearfully from face to face. None were talking.

"Just look at her!" someone cried near the cockroach sorters. "The nerve to come in here by herself. Where's Pester?"

Another shouted from across the warehouse, where workers filled flour sacks, "Make sure she doesn't try lifting a different bag. The point is to try to starve her out."

Nia dropped her sack and backed away in terror. As she did, a strange light came into view overhead. It was faint, but the memory of Tanni returned. His light was just as beautifully bright. Her thoughts were interrupted by a soft, distinctly feminine voice.

"Can you hear me?" it asked. "I'm trying to open a channel with you."

Nia's legs gave way. She still heard the other voices, which continued joking about her. Apparently, they'd not heard the question. *I can,* she thought. *Are you the voice I've been missing? I don't recall it sounding so gentle.*

A chuckle like a tinkling bell echoed over the other voices, "No, dear. I'm one who wishes to help you. Do you really want to carry that flour sack there? It looks rather too big for you."

If I don't carry it, I don't eat, Nia thought incredulously.

The voice didn't reply, so Nia grabbed the flour sack and attempted to shoulder it. But the weight was too much. Her legs gave away, and the bag pinned her to the ground. The mocking laughter grew louder as Nia lay panting on the floor.

"They want you to die here," the voice said mournfully. "They no longer see any use for you. To them you are but a small and insignificant nuisance, hardly worth their notice."

Tears stung Nia's eyes. *They're not wrong. That's what I am. That's all I am—a burden, a big nuisance to those around me.*

"Nonsense!" cried the voice sternly. "You carry so much value that these imps are terrified of you. They're terrified because you have the strength within yourself to annihilate their whole world. You even carry the power to set their Starbeams free."

I do?

"Yes, you do," the voice exhaled softly. "Listen, you wondered a few minutes ago who decides to live like this. No one does. It's forced upon them like it was forced upon you. Without someone like you to set things right, all will die from it eventually. As for the imps, they care only for the physically strongest, who alone are permitted to live as mere shadows in this twisted realm."

Imps?

"Yes. Those things you've sensed on the shoulders of your fellow Shadians. You have one too, though currently he sleeps."

Nia clenched her fists until the knuckles turned white. She wanted to break something, but panic threatened to debilitate her. *How do I escape him?* she asked desperately. *What should I do before he wakes up?*

"You seek my advice? Funny, Tanni never has. Very well, listen to me very closely."

The other voices raged on, lobbing insult after insult. Nia closed her eyes to focus.

"If you want to escape your imp," the kind voice continued, "you'll first need to rescue Tanni. He's being kept in the house nearest the warehouse. If you succeed in helping him escape, you'll free me as well, and I'll be able to keep your imp from reclaiming you. I might even be able to get you out of the Shadelands and back into the Sunlands where you're from."

The excitement of leaving the Shadelands lasted only a moment. Then, Nia's heart sank, and she felt very small. *You want me to rescue Tanni? Won't that be dangerous?*

"If such a path sounds too dangerous, get yourself out of here as quick as you can and don't look back. But be forewarned that even with a head start your imp will rise soon, and no doubt he'll be able to find you within an hour of his waking. If he does, resist him with all the strength you have, even if you must die in the process. Life was never meant to be spent in darkness."

Nia released the flour bag. She ground her teeth at the

ridiculous laughter of the unseen imps, then stared at the light, allowing its dull warmth to wash over her.

Something sparked within her—a fire she'd long forgotten. Leaping to her feet, she glared defiantly at the menacing form on the new miller's shoulder. It hissed. Nia drew in a deep breath and marched away without a backward glance.

Once outside, she went to the nearest house, grabbed the handle, and pulled. It was locked. Balling her hands into fists, she moved to the window and peered in. Tanni was stretched out on a surprisingly clean floor, but his appearance had changed dramatically. His light was gone, and his face was caked in dirt. His once beautiful tunic was filthy and torn.

"Tanni!" Nia called, pounding on the window. "Tanni, wake up! I'm here to free you." Tanni didn't move. Going to the door, she continued to pound. Then, it opened, without as much as a squeak. She sprang inside, unwary of such things as traps. Instantly, the door slammed shut behind her. Tanni leapt to his feet with a rope in hand, snatched at her wrist, and tried to bind it.

"Tanni, let go! What are you doing? You're a Starbeam!" Nia cried, tearing free of his grasp and rushing for the door. It was locked. Vertical bars lined the interior like a giant cage. Tanni slammed her into them and began lashing one of her wrists to the bars.

A flashback of an angry cat springing at Nia flooded her memory, followed by her knocking it into a pile of straw. The memory was fresh as the day it happened.

"Tanni, I'm very sorry about this," Nia panted. Then, mimicking what she did to the cat, she pivoted her free elbow into Tanni's face, sending him flying back into a ruined dresser. "Come at me again and I'll knock you out cold."

The boy lay in a heap. Nia wondered if she really did knock him out. When he sat up, the start of a black eye appeared on his dirt smeared face. "Nia?" he moaned, regaining his composure.

"Nia, is that you? Why did you just hit me?"

Nia opened her mouth to answer, but a sinister voice cut her off, saying, "You'll pay for waking him up."

Nia's blood curdled. The air grew darker and colder. Her ears popped from the dropping atmospheric pressure. The whole shack began to shake. Tanni cowered against the wall as an ominous black shadow descended from the rafters heading Nia's way. A scream caught in her throat.

But at that moment, the shack burst with a light that exploded from Tanni's body. It shattered the cottage window and blasted open the cottage door. The shadow gave a piercing shriek before disappearing into the rafters. Stunned, Nia felt something pushing against her. It was Tanni shoving her out the door. A fleeting form appeared outside the shack, but it fled at Tanni's brightness. Weaving past Shadians on the path, Nia and Tanni broke free and headed for the woods. A pair of beady eyes watched them go.

CHAPTER 6

Pester awakened dizzy and disoriented. Blinking to clear his vision, he felt nourishing yet unsatisfying energy wash over him. It left him strangely irritated. Frowning, he sat up to take in his surroundings. The room was run down and filthy. Fleas hopped all around him but seemed unwilling to touch him. Garbage was everywhere.

Someone is a poor housekeeper, he thought in bemusement. Then, he remembered a girl maneuvering over the rubbish. *Oh yes, that poor housekeeper is me. Go figure.*

Hopping from the head of Nia's ruined bed to her nightstand, Pester rubbed his temples and wracked his brain. Imps rarely slept. They didn't need to. Why then had he been lying there?

Finally, he chuckled, "Oh yes, the healing spell. Glad I'm not dust after that one."

He slapped his thighs and laughed in relief. But a moment later, he stiffened. His mouth hung open as he scanned the cottage. No Nia. "Is she dead?" he questioned. "Did someone come and remove her body to the edge of town? No, she's alive. I can feel her energy. She's wandered off somewhere in the village. Brilliant," he muttered. "Now, I have to go find her."

Pester flew clumsily through the rafters and crawled through the trap door. Then, he relied on his inner sense to search for her from the rooftop. At first, he drew a blank. Something strange and foreign blocked him from seeing clearly. A moment later, his eyes popped open. Nia was at the warehouse, and the imprisoned sprite was interfering with his connection. Angrily, he pushed off the roof and toward the girl he hoped to get away from "that conniving, nasty sprite."

When Pester reached the imp's doorway above the main door taken by the Shadians, Nia was nowhere to be seen. Instead, he overheard several imps joking from their drudges' shoulders about how long it would take the girl to starve to death. *So, every imp in Shades wants her dead?* Pester's stomach went cold. *This doesn't bode well.* Such coarse talk would never have been exchanged at the mines. Even the puniest mine drudge was too valuable to discard, assuming they were healthy.

Maybe now that she's older, the mine imps won't turn her down again. She could be useful as a camp cook, thought Pester.

He was turning to leave when a light blasted through the warehouse. *Oh no,* he thought. *Not again!*

Imps exploded into dust on impact. Windows shattered throughout the building. The blast's searing heat shot Pester through the warehouse doorway into a pile of rotten flour across the lane.

When will the carnage end? Pester shivered. Bruised and covered in rancid insect flour, he dug himself out just as Nia, Tanni, and the sprite rushed through the streets of Shades and into the forest. Pester's heart sank as he watched his energy source scurry away.

Besides himself, few noticed the escaping trio. Shades' other imps were in a state of shock. No one moved from their drudge's shoulders or spoke. But as Vex appeared alive but shaken on the roof of his house, a general hiss of anger broke out and a mob of imps charged his way.

"Stop! What are you doing?" Vex bellowed over the clamor of accusations.

"This is all Pester and your fault!" roared Addle. At this, Pester squirmed his way back into the flour, unaware of live cockroaches scuttling away from him.

"You all are crazy!" Vex shouted. "Blame Pester. How's it my fault?"

"We allowed you to lead us into danger by capturing the sprite and her Starbeam. We've suffered casualties because you wanted to torture the sprite instead of killing her. Half the drudges in town are sick because of that boy," Addle cried. "Now, Pester's drudge has set him and the sprite loose again."

Pester peeked out cautiously. Imps nearby picked up trash and tools to throw at Vex. Shouts of "Traitor!" filled the air.

"I told you," Vex hissed, "the only casualties are on Pester's head. Kill him!"

Pester's blood ran cold as the entire town took up the chant for his blood. Mere feet from his hiding spot, Addle, who sat on his tall, muscular drudge, raised a crooked hand. The town quieted.

"What you've done equally merits death," Addle said, his eyebrows furrowed. "You're an Original, Vex. Surely, you're aware that if the sprite had been properly disposed of, Daze and all the other mill imps would be alive right now."

"Pester controls Nia's actions. Turn your wrath against him and his drudge. If they hadn't been so meddling," Vex growled, "no one would have gotten hurt."

The air filled with shouts of, "Liar!"

"Enough!" Addle crossed his arms. "Look, I'd remove your head myself, but everyone knows you're too good of friends with Lord Accuse. No one would dare set a claw against you. That said, you've entirely worn out your welcome. Get out!" The town echoed Addle's last statement. Vex pleaded with the town imps to settle down and not make rash decisions. This only aggravated the mob, and they yelled "Get out!" all the louder.

It was the perfect moment to escape. Pester peered at the imps and drudges near his rancid flour pile. Nearly every imp was focused on Vex. Shaking the rotten flour off, Pester silently flew in the direction the children and sprite had escaped. Three blocks from the town center, he rounded a bend—and ran right into his sister, Taunt. Her back was to him, but she spun around. Their eyes met. Pester felt he was going to be sick.

"Ugh!" Taunt eyed Pester with characteristic disgust and hatred. She sniffed the air. "You look disgusting, and you stink. What are you covered in?"

"None of your business," Pester said. In the distance, the crowd renewed their shouts to find and kill him. He fidgeted and inched away from his sister.

"Getting out of dodge, brother? Too cowardly to face the mob? I knew you were weak," Taunt teased, "but this is a new low for you."

"You know that mob is only looking for blood. So yes, I'm getting out of here."

"Oh ho, not if I tell them you're here. I've waited a long time for this!" Taunt laughed. Flashing a nasty grin with soiled teeth, she cupped clawed hands around her mouth and prepared to shout.

Pester lunged at his sister. Tackling her, he covered her mouth. Taunt sank her teeth into his hand as they rolled through the coal dusted dirt. Pester bit back a scream and pinned Taunt beneath him. Then, he repositioned his hand to cover her nose as well.

"You and Wither have wanted me dead since we were in the nest. If it hadn't been for mother's determined protection, I probably already would be. But we're not implings anymore. Did you forget? We're legally considered family now." Pester's mouth twitched with rage. His hand remained in place on her face. "The law specifically prohibits outright killing or committing an action that leads to the death of a family member. The imps of Shades could all back up your murderous deed, but our magic will know what you did to me. Do you really want your magical abilities to vanish? If so, go ahead and shout. Just thought I'd give you a fair warning first." He then yanked his bleeding hand from her mouth.

Taunt spat in his face. "Fine," she said. "Get out."

Pester stood up. He peeked around the building at the distant crowds. They were still shouting for blood, but they didn't know where he was—yet.

"Believe me, sister, I intend to. And I may never return."

"Don't call me *sister*. Don't call me anything. You were to blame for mother's death. I never want to see your ugly, little face again."

"Mother died trying to heal all three of us, not just me, remember?" Pester snarled. "If you'd been the last to be healed instead of me, the blame would be on your head, wouldn't it? Think about it for a minute. And trust me. I hope to go several lifetimes without seeing your ugly, little face again. May this be the final time we ever have to speak to each other again."

Leaping into the air, he fled from his sister and the screaming crowd and sped after the children. He had a drudge to catch.

CHAPTER 7

Hands on their knees, Nia and Tanni gasped for air. They didn't know how long they'd been running, and they had no idea where they were. Panting, Nia peered around the dark, acrid forest. It was littered with dead branches and coal dust, illuminated faintly by Tanni's light. She would have been glad of the light, if she didn't have the distinct sense the trees were watching them.

"No!" she cried in response to a memory of endless days spent lost and hungry. "What have I done?"

Tanni caught his breath and straightened up. "What's wrong?"

"How could I bring you here? Tanni, you can't imagine what a nuisance I'll soon be to you. This is just like the time I entered the Shadelands and ran into a lady who didn't know her way through the trees. I told her I did and tried leading her out the way I'd come. We were getting nowhere, and she was getting more and more angry with me. Finally, she told me I wasn't worth the trouble—that she'd find her own way out." Nia shivered and rubbed her arms. "She was right. I wasn't worth the trouble. I never found a way out of these woods. Don't burden yourself with me. I'm a terrible guide!"

"Nia!" Tanni's light pulsated as he spoke. "It doesn't matter if you know your way out or not. I don't expect that of you. The lady who did was crazy to demand so much out of you. You were what, five? No one in their right mind would abandon a child like that. And, if it hadn't been for you, I'd still be under the control of the cruelest imp in the Shadelands. Think about it. Where else other than the woods would you bring me? That shabby town is surrounded by these trees."

"The lady had a perfectly good reason to abandon me. My presence tends to irritate people." Nia lowered her eyes as she said this. "You look irritated yourself." She stood lifeless and dejected like the Shadians she'd just left behind.

Tanni took a few calming breaths. At last, he said evenly, "Nia, you don't irritate me. Imps do. It irritates me that they would lie to you so long and lead you to think you weren't worth anyone's time. The Lumen calls them the Parents of Lies for a reason."

"What's a Lumen?" asked Nia dully.

"The Lumen is a man. He's my instructor. He shines without the help of sprites, so he's been given a special title," Tanni explained.

"What are sprites?" asked Nia in confusion.

"They're shining beings that make Starbeams—well, Starbeams," Tanni clarified. "I can't see mine or hear her most of the time, but The Lumen says I have one. He told me her name was Ease."

"Ah. Now I know who was speaking to me in town." Nia continued staring at the ground, her voice cheerless. "Thank you, Ease."

"Wait! You've heard her?" Tanni cried, his light brightening in excitement.

"Sure," Nia said dejectedly. "She's the one who told me to save you. Now you're saved. I think that's all the use I was good for. Now that I've served my purpose, it's probably best not to trouble yourself with me any further."

"You are not a burden!" Ease insisted.

Tanni balled his hands into fists. "Nia, don't listen to imps. Your value doesn't come from whether or not you can perform their useless tasks. Listen to me," he said. "You're coming with me. We're going to find a way out of here. You're going to be rid of this place once and for all."

Despite Tanni's optimism, Nia remained disconsolate. Tanni placed a hand on her shoulder. "As I said before, you have parents who've been looking for you for a long time." His voice softened, "Wouldn't it be great to see them again?"

Nia shrugged, "I'd only be in their way. Mom needs a quiet household so she can take care of the baby." Her voice was small, like a young, lost child.

After an awkward pause, Tanni gave Nia's shoulder a squeeze. "I had no idea being here would give you such a false perspective of time. Your mother's baby is your younger sister, Rosa. She's seven now. There's no way your presence would make the house any more or less boisterous than it already is. Besides, I know Rosa. She feels cheated. Cheated out of having an older sister."

Nia's face felt hot. She looked up at Tanni's faintly glowing eyes. They were brown, like she remembered hers to be. Warmth and sympathy shone through them.

"I have a younger sister who knows about me?" She asked breathlessly.

"Yes," Tanni said with a smile. "She often draws pictures of the two of you holding hands. Your parents have described you to her to the last detail."

Tears started in Nia's eyes. "I have a sister," she said, her heart full.

Tanni grinned, then reddened and turned hastily away from her. He rubbed the curly, black hair on the back of his head. After a few moments of deliberating, he cleared his throat and said bravely, "Since I haven't eaten a real meal in a few days, how about we go find my food pack? Then we can talk about how in stars we're gonna rescue ourselves."

"You really think we can get out of here?" Something like hope broke into Nia's bleakness.

"I make no promises," Tanni said, hands in the air, "but I'll give it a shot."

Longing for the sister she never knew, Nia followed Tanni deeper into the trees. In the warmth of his smile, she'd momentarily forgotten about the darkness surrounding her. Now, it felt doubly oppressive. The forbidding bows of the trees seemed plagued with watching eyes.

***

If Pester thought it would be easy following the children, he was wrong. He hadn't realized how strong sprite concealment magic could be against one imp. When flanked by the adult imps in Shades, Nia's trail was so easy to follow it was laughable. But this—this was hopeless. The trees only offered vague echoes of the children's direction.

"A fine lot of spies you all are," Pester said. "I thought you were controlled by Lord Accuse's finest magic. If I don't figure out a way to track Nia through you, I may as well be dead."

He wandered for several more minutes, when suddenly, he heard a voice behind him that froze him to his bones. "Going somewhere, Pester?"

Turning around, he saw Vex. The larger imp looked murderous.

"Wait, Vex!" Pester sputtered, looking in vain for an escape. "What happened back there in town wasn't my fault."

"No?" said Vex, his voice dangerously soft. "What was that healing spell residue on your drudge, then? I don't recall being the one to cast it." As Vex spoke, he advanced toward Pester, who slowly backed away.

"I—I wanted to see if I could at least try it. I didn't know it would lead to this. Please, Vex, please, let me fix this."

"Fix this?" Vex hissed, baring his teeth. "Can you fix a whole town banishing me? Can you recapture a Starbeam guarded by a sprite, who's now loose in the Shadelands and ready to wreak havoc on everything I helped Lord Accuse build? Wretched, weak little traitor! I'll kill you for this!"

Vex charged. Pester scrambled away and backed right into a tree. Before he could get around it, Vex was on him. He grabbed Pester by the throat and raised a clawed hand for the killing blow. In panic, Pester screamed, "You're right, Vex, I am weak!"

Caught by surprise, a sneer formed on Vex's face. His hand hung in the air. "What did you say?"

"I'm weak! I'm a sorry excuse for an imp. I'm not worthy to be in the shadow of your greatness!"

For a long, suspenseful moment, Vex glared at him. Then he dropped Pester and roared with laughter. "Pester the jester," he crowed between guffaws. Pester cowered. "I'll give you this much at least. You do have the uncanny ability to amuse me. It almost makes me regret killing you."

"If you like laughter, you'll love the mines," said Pester, trembling. "The sprite is strong, but if we work together, we can weaken her magic, and I could get you a new life as a mine imp. The Starbeam boy would make a fine mine drudge."

Scratching his chin thoughtfully, Vex asked, "How could a little pip squeak like you possibly help to weaken the sprite's magic?"

"There's a certain lullaby my mother taught me that's worked on Nia for years. I can teach it to you."

Vex crossed his arms and growled, "But how would we get close enough to use this lullaby?"

"The trees could sing it," Pester gulped.

Vex's eyes narrowed, "Pester, you are on dangerous ground. But, if you can do all that you say you can, I may just refrain from killing you. You can start by teaching this tree your song. Let's see how effective it is in revealing the sprite's location."

Nodding in relief, Pester pushed himself to his feet and turned toward the tree. He squeezed his eyes shut and started to sing.

CHAPTER 8

This isn't bread!" Nia stared at a lightly tanned flat cake in her hand. Tanni laughed and playfully demanded what was wrong with the food. "It's the wrong color," Nia said, turning the large oval over in her hands. "And the texture, the texture is all wrong."

"It isn't made of garbage, anyway," Tanni grinned. "Try it."

Nia frowned, "Our bread isn't made of garbage. It's made of cockroach flour."

"Ugh!" Tanni pretended to vomit. "That may be even worse! Look, Nia. Tear off a piece, put a chunk of dried fruit or some pine nuts on it, and take a bite. Don't turn your nose up at food after so many days of not eating. The bread's pretty stale, but it's still plenty edible."

Letting out a sigh, Nia followed Tanni's suggestion. To her surprise, the pine nuts were strangely satisfying.

"I'd forgotten food could be tasty," she said, imitating Tanni and shoving bread chunks and dried fruit into her cheeks.

"You two look like chipmunks," Ease chortled. Seeing Nia's blank look she quickly explained what a chipmunk was.

Satiated, Nia sat in tranquil satisfaction. With her eyes closed, she asked Tanni why he decided to come to the Shadelands.

"I told you already," said Tanni, picking something out of his teeth. "The Lumen only entered the Shadelands to bring back people who hadn't been caught by imps yet. I thought this to be cowardice, so I packed my things, left him a note, and opened a portal to the Shadelands. The portal's where I intend to bring you next."

"Good," said Nia, opening her eyes to stare at the unfriendly trees. "But why did you choose me? To rescue, I mean. There was more than one kid in the town. I'm sure you saw them."

Tanni's cheeks colored faintly. But his steady voice gave nothing away. "You looked like your mind was more awake than the others."

"Mostly," said Nia pensively. "But you found me when I was most determined not to think."

"Really?" Tanni asked earnestly. "Why?"

Nia sighed, "Loneliness was eating me alive. I'd just come from the well where I'd been waiting for a drink of water. I thought it was my turn, but then two others cut right in front of me. I can't blame them, though. As you've probably noticed, I'm usually in the way."

"Nia, we've been through this. You're not—"

Tanni was interrupted by a haunting lullaby echoing through the trees.

> *You've ended your thoughts, now your troubles sleep.*
> *In my arms your fears I keep.*
> *My voice is your guide, your mind set aside.*
> *Through the endless night, I'm your reason, I'm your light.*
> *All your worries have died, you are satisfied.*
> *Yes, you are satisfied.*

Nia's eyes were wide with alarm. "I know that song," she said in a near whisper. "This isn't good."

"What is—it?" Tanni slurred. His eyes crossed.

"Tell Tanni to plug his ears!" Ease cried. "We need to get out of here—now!"

But the boy was already under the song's spell. His hands were limp at his side, his expression blank. Nia covered Tanni's ears herself and pulled him away from the singing tree. As if the musical spell broke, he came to and clawed frantically at her hands.

"Stop!" Nia screamed. "Tanni, plug your ears quickly! Ease says you must!"

The song began a third time. Hands cupped over his ears, Tanni opened his mouth to speak, but all that came out was a startled squeak. The tree they stood under groaned and swayed, its gnarled branches reaching out to grab them. Other trees did the same.

"My magic's weakening. We're being located!" Ease tugged invisibly on the front of Nia's ragged tunic. "We've got to get going now!"

Grabbing Tanni's pack, Nia pulled at the boy's sleeve. Together, the two ran, dodging tree branches that reached toward them and jumping over tree roots that raised suddenly in unexpected places. All at once, they were on the ground, sprawled out face down. The root that tripped them stretched over the back of their legs and came down, pinning their legs underneath it. The song continued, and Tanni's glow steadily diminished.

"Ease!" Nia screamed. "That's your light, isn't it? Why are you darkening? Where are you?"

"I'm right here, Nia. I'm in front of you."

"Help us!" Nia reached toward the voice but found only pine needles.

"I can't help unless this stops," Ease said, her voice thick with grief.

"Well, stop it then!"

"I can't. I've never felt an energy like this before."

The root pressed hard against Nia. Others attempted to grab her arms. "Then what can I do to stop it?" she shouted.

"You can't," Ease sobbed. "You need my light."

"Fine!" Nia gritted her teeth. The pain was almost unbearable. "How can I make you glow again?"

"I need joy. I need happy energy. Tanni," Ease began faintly, "has almost none to give."

Nia struggled against the root, but it was no use. Tanni lay beside her, eyes open, face expressionless. "Can't you use mine?" she whimpered.

"Dear child, if you had any happiness at all, I'd use it."

Desperate, Nia closed her eyes in hopes of recalling a single memory when she'd been truly happy; a time before the Shadelands. As the incessant singing continued and her leg was slowly crushed, she remembered the day her father finally let her into his blacksmith shop. She was five at the time. The heavy clanging and the ringing, rhythmic *ting, ting* of a hammer on glowing metal filled her with wonder and pride. Best of all, her father handed her a tiny hammer he made specially for her, along with a small block of steel, and let her bang away to her heart's content while he continued his work.

For a moment, a warm, happy smile spread across Nia's face. It was enough. A white burst of light shot out of her, cracking in half the tree root that held her and Tanni. Overhead, the trees stopped swaying. The lullaby quieted to a mere whisper. Opening her eyes, Nia saw a small and lovely female form in front of her. Then, the figure vanished. Nia stared at her arms as the residual light faded back into darkness.

"Ow, my head!" Tanni was awake again, rubbing his temples. "Was that really your imp's lullaby? It sounded awful."

"Yes, it was my imp's," Nia said sheepishly. "We've got to get away from here. Ease thinks we've been located."

"The singing is still going," Tanni said. "I don't think these trees will hide us."

"We need to get to the portal," Ease said.

Nia nodded. She climbed to her feet and lifted Tanni to his. "You and Ease keep mentioning a portal. Is that a door or something?"

"Yes, of sorts. It's a magical rift between two realms," Tanni grimaced. Messaging the back of his head, he continued, "If someone in the Sunlands were to go through it, they'd end up here. If a Shadian were to use it, they'd end up there."

"So in theory, anyone on this side should be able to go through it, regardless of how long they've been here?"

Tanni nodded.

"Then what are we waiting for?" Nia asked impatiently. "Let's go!"

CHAPTER 9

Pester's mind raced. Whatever magic he might have used against Vex had been channeled into the trunk of a tree. If he wanted to survive, his next words were critical. Vex hadn't indicated whether he'd given over killing him. Rather, it seemed he was biding his time until he knew where the children had gone. If Pester played his hand too soon, Vex would have no further use of him and dispatch him quickly. No amount of further groveling would then stay the ancient imp's murderous wrath.

"So?" asked Vex, the evenness of his voice belying his cruel intentions. "Where are they?"

"They're over that way," Pester said steadily, pointing past Vex.

"Over what way?" Vex demanded. "Where exactly did you find them?"

"It wouldn't matter where exactly they were located, because they most certainly would have moved on by the time you got there," said Pester, his palms clammy. "It would be in your best interest if we go in the direction that I felt them for five minutes and then recheck with the trees to see if we're still going the right way."

Vex snarled and punched the tree next to Pester's head. Pester flinched. "Swear on every curse you're not lying to me."

"I swear," Pester replied, willing his knocking knees to still.

"Curse you!" Vex exhaled. "Lead on then. But lead me astray, and I'll give you such a slow and painful death you'll wish you never hatched."

I'd do the same to you in a heartbeat, Pester thought with a nod, flying away in the direction of his drudge. Vex followed close behind, breathing murderous threats down his neck.

***

"Tell me a bit about your family," Nia said to Tanni as they hunted for the portal. "How many are there in it? I hope I'm not bugging you too much by asking."

"You're not bugging me," said Tanni. "I come from a family of four, like you. My dad's a baker. He makes some of the most amazing pastries. That's actually how I got the bread for this trip. Mom's a weaver—you know, one who makes cloth. She's really good at it. In some ways she almost earns more money from the market selling her wares than dad makes selling his bread. The tunic I'm wearing came from her."

"That's amazing," Nia said, suddenly embarrassed of her own tattered tunic. His mother would probably balk to see it.

"I know, right?" Oblivious to Nia's self-consciousness, Tanni tugged on the edge of his long shirt. "I plan to wash and mend it when we get home. Would be a shame to lose it. But yeah, thanks to the hard work of my parents we live a pretty good life out in the country. We moved to the township of Thistlespray about five years ago."

"The home of my parents!" Nia exclaimed.

Tanni laughed, "Yep, exactly. Fiddi, my older brother, was the first to introduce himself to them. He was eight at the time, and I was seven."

58

"How old are you now?" asked Nia, turning red at her forwardness. Again, he didn't notice her discomfort.

"I'm just three months shy of thirteen. Fiddi just turned fourteen, and he's full of himself. You know how old you are, don't you?" Nia shook her head. "You're twelve and a half. Your birthday is in five and a half months."

"Is it?"

"Yep. But anyway, back when we met your family, Rosa was just a toddler. Fiddi and I used to like making her laugh."

"Wish I could have made her laugh too," Nia muttered to herself, her sense of loneliness building.

"You still have time. She's only seven, after all, and she still loves giggling just as much," Tanni said cheerfully. "Over the years my family has remained close to yours. For two years they laughed along with us and acted pretty happy, but I always noticed a sadness under the surface."

"Why?" asked Nia, her heart aching. "Why were they. . ." She trailed off. Clearing the lump in her throat, she finally said, "Why were they sad?"

"Because they didn't have you," said Tanni, facing Nia.

Nia stopped walking. Her breath caught in her throat and her cheeks felt very warm. "They were sad because they didn't have me?" she asked incredulously.

"Yes," said Tanni. He tilted his head. "Why wouldn't they be?"

"Are you sure they weren't sad about something else?"

"Absolutely, and I'll tell you why. One day I got the nerve up to ask them about their sadness. Your mom was hesitant to answer, but your dad took out a drawing of you that a local artist did when you were five. Your dad said, 'Here's why. We lost the most precious angel in Sunburst—besides Rosa, of course.' He then shared the story of your grandmother taking you while your mom was delivering your sister, and how your Nanna still hates herself for causing you to run off." Tanni rubbed his chin thoughtfully and pursed his lips. "You do remember that incident, don't you?"

"Like it was yesterday," said Nia, fighting back tears. "Why would Nanna hate herself for chasing me away? She had every right to say what she did to me."

"You realize she spoke those words out of stress, don't you? Your Nanna loves you, Nia."

Nia grabbed at her matted hair and shook her head vigorously. There was no way her Nanna didn't think her a nuisance. Just look at the sickness she had brought on her, and the block that injured her! *Thoughtful children don't do things like that. Thoughtful children don't run off and ignore their grandmother's pleas to stop, either.*

"Nia?" Tanni asked quietly. His expression was serious. She looked up at him. He gave her a scrutinizing look. "You blame yourself for what happened, don't you?"

Looking away, her shoulders slumped, she slowly nodded.

"What all do you blame yourself for?"

"For causing Nanna's pain. For a thousand other mistakes I've made since that day."

"Such as what?" asked Tanni, his mouth frowning.

Nia's voice shook as she replied, "I'm always in everyone's way. I've always been such a hassle. Like that time I wasn't looking where I was going and accidentally knocked a lady into the town well in Shades. She had to be fished out. A man whipped my back because of it, and the door to my shack was locked for a whole day to keep me out of trouble. Or that time I nearly starved a stray cat to death, because I didn't know it needed meat and not bread. It finally escaped and ran off into the woods. Everything I've done has led to grief for others. I'm such a terrible, terrible nuisance. I can't take it anymore. I can't take it!"

Tanni put his hands firmly on Nia's shoulders. "It was your imp who wasn't watching out for you the day you knocked the lady into the well. It was his fault, not yours. He certainly didn't alert you to it, did he? And trying to help the cat shows you're a kindhearted person. No one can fault you because you didn't know what to feed it. I most certainly don't. Stop blaming yourself for every little mishap that takes place around you."

"How can I not?" asked Nia miserably.

"Because, as I told you," Tanni insisted, "it's not your fault. So, listen, about an hour from here is the portal. When you see it, you're going to go through it, and you're going to leave behind this guilt that you've been carrying around for so many years. You're going to hug your grandmother, and she's going to hold you and say she's never going to let you go. You hear?"

Nia wiped away a tear and stood still. A gentle voice spoke in her ear. It was Ease. "Come, child," she said. "I'll help you walk the rest of the way."

Peace washed over Nia. She breathed in slowly, deeply, and met Tanni's eyes again. "You both are so kind to me. I don't deserve it."

"Yes, you do," said Tanni, the words a healing balm on her soul. "Ease, you know where the portal is. Lead us the rest of the way to it."

A light appeared abruptly in front of them.

"Ready, Nia?" Tanni asked.

Still under Ease's calming spell, Nia began the last leg of the journey, with only a slight hesitation remaining somewhere in the back of her mind.

CHAPTER 10

The sun was setting. Tanni's spirits were rising, in spite of the never-ending lullaby and the watchful, forbidding trees. As Tanni explained, he'd nearly completed his personal quest to save a Shadian. He couldn't wait to see The Lumen's face when he and Nia walked together to the other side.

"Oh man, Fiddi's gonna be so jealous," he chuckled, practically dancing.

"Why would he be jealous?" Nia asked, trying to ignore her growing nervousness.

"He's my older brother. He reminds me of that fact almost daily," Tanni said, rolling his eyes. "He likes being the one all the cool stuff happens to. But now I'll have something to hold over his head for a change. You should just hear all his talk about how being a teenager has made him so much wiser than he used to be. 'Tanni,' he says, 'when you're a teenager, you'll understand just how much the adults don't actually know.' Well, now I'll be able to say I know even more than The Lumen himself."

Just ahead, Ease let out an exaggerated sigh. Nia started to ask why Tanni's statement offended the sprite, when a wave of cold air washed over her. A foreboding sense of dread made her cower in place. Tanni stopped sniggering. He scanned to the left and right nervously. The dark feeling was almost palpable. An icy wind whipped through the forest, sending the tree branches into a frenzy. Tanni grabbed Nia from behind and held her before him like a human shield.

"Nia," he whispered, "what is that? What's happening?"

Tanni's light faded away and was replaced by twilight. Through the darkness, Nia's breath came out in frozen puffs. Her heart hammered in her chest.

"Nia," said Ease, her voice frightened and strained. "I need you and Tanni to go as quietly as you can and hide in the bushes. Do you see them? They're to your left."

"Ease, what's going on?" Nia asked.

"The lord of this world is coming. The portal is drawing him. Go!" the sprite urged. "He's almost here."

Nia snatched Tanni's right hand from her shoulder and pulled him toward the bushes Ease had indicated. Wordlessly, he followed her lead. Hiding amid the bushes' thorny canes,. the children crouched and waited. They hardly dared to breathe. The feeling of dread deepened, as did the darkness. Nia was simultaneously relieved and unnerved at the absence of light shining from Tanni. He now looked ordinary, like a Shadian.

A tense, quiet moment passed. Then, a sound reverberated through Nia's head: voices. Turning to face them, she sensed shadows moving to a slightly brighter spot between two trees. The shadows were no more than thirty yards away. *The bright spot is Ease!* Nia thought, her mouth going dry. *The sprite is doomed! I must help her. I have to stop them from catching my friend!*

A dark voice shouted, its tone as deep as the lowest note on a pipe organ, "Curses! Here's the portal. I knew I sensed one. What idiot Starbeam opens a portal and then fails to close it behind them when they leave?"

"My Lord Accuse," squeaked a second voice Nia sensed

belonged to a female, "if I may, I don't sense any sign of reentry."

"What do you mean, Prattle?"

"Look at it carefully, sir," Prattle said. "Whoever entered hasn't left the Shadelands yet."

"Ugh!" cried a gravelly male voice. "As much as I hate saying it, I think she's right, my lord. And I sense something else. Whoever cast this portal was fairly young and inexperienced. There was also only one of them."

Lord Accuse grunted, "Did you get a sense of how powerful this Starbeam was, Ire?"

"Pretty weak, sir, judging by the instability of this portal," Ire cackled.

"But, my lord, you are going to close it, aren't you?" Prattle squeaked. "Weak or not, Starbeams sometimes carry sprites around with them, and if that sprite is allowed to leave the Shadelands, who knows what damage they could do—knowing where our own weaknesses are and how to exploit them, and—"

"Silence! I'm well aware of the dangers a sprite poses," Lord Accuse snarled. "Besides, I may be able to use this to my advantage. Somewhere in the Shadelands a sprite may be desperate to get home. The promise of safety is a powerful lure. Ire, you specialize in deception magic. Convert this portal into a trap. Let's see what sort of fish our net catches."

"Yes, sir," said Ire.

Nia's stomach knotted as the portal's color changed ever so slightly.

Ire took a step back and gestured grandly toward the modified portal. "The trap," he said, "is set, sir."

"Is it escapable?"

"No, my lord. It's still a portal, but now it leads to one of your dungeon cages. Nothing going in will ever get out again. You'll be able to deal with them at your leisure."

"Good," said Lord Accuse. "As they say, a watched cage catches no birds. I've just realized we're not far from the town of Shades, and I'm keen to check in on a friend of mine. He goes by the name of Vex, and he practically runs the place. Perhaps he knows something more of this reckless Starbeam brat. If the youngster did have a sprite with him and Vex got word of it, the wretch may be dead already. Only one sure way to find out."

"But sir, what if the sprite does get caught in here? What do you plan to do with it?" Prattle asked anxiously.

"Feed you to it and listen to your screams!" Lord Accuse laughed menacingly. Ire cackled. "No, Prattle," the imp lord said soberly. "If the sprite gets caught and is transferred to my dungeon, I'm sure I'll get to it eventually— in the next ten years or so. For now, to Shades."

As the voices of the three imps grew fainter, the air lightened a bit and grew warmer. A faint glow emanated from Tanni.

"What was that?" Tanni wondered with a shudder.

"The imp lord and two others were here," Nia said, her body aching from fear. "Didn't you see or hear them?"

"I saw them," Tanni said, "but I didn't hear them."

"Oh Nia, I'm so, so sorry." Ease sounded as low as Nia felt.

Shaking away his jitters, Tanni crawled out of the thorny bushes, wearing a dumb smile. "They're gone! I don't know about you, but I'd like to get out of this nasty place. Shall we go through the portal?"

Ease audibly groaned. Nia smacked herself on the forehead.

"What?" asked Tanni.

"Didn't you see what just happened?" asked Nia.

"What do you mean?" Tanni crouched down to Nia's level.

"We—we can't go through the portal," Nia said numbly.

"What?" cried Tanni. "The portal is right there! Don't make me drag you through it."

"No need," Nia whispered. "It won't take us to the Sunlands anymore. The imps have changed it."

Tanni's mouth hung open. "They changed it?" he asked. "How? What did they turn it into?"

Shuddering, Nia answered, "A trap."

CHAPTER 11

It was fully dark beneath the canopy when Pester stopped yet again to gather the children's direction. It had been slow going thus far. Wherever the sprite was, she was using her magic to counter his spell and send false readings. As a result, he was hard pressed to find Nia's true location, and was forced instead to sift through a cacophony of misleading information. He'd worked throughout the day without a single break, as if his life depended on it—which it did.

Pressing his long, pointy ear against a tree's bark, Pester held his breath and listened. Nothing came—no sound at all. His heart sank. Something had interfered with his song.

"You know, Pester," Vex yawned irritably, "I've been thinking. Your nest mother gave you the wrong name. Shouldn't you have been called Lull? You're taking so long you're lulling me to sleep."

Pester bristled, "I wasn't named Lull because it was already taken. That was my mother's name."

"Wait, Lull was your mother?" Vex asked, humor in his voice. "The Original Lull? Isn't that rich? She always was very tiresome. Yes, she used to make me yawn considerably. No wonder being around you is so draining."

Rage coursed through Pester, but he stifled it. "You know," he hissed, "if I drain you so much, there's a sturdy branch up there in the canopy. Settle down and take a nap if you're so tired." Vex took a menacing step toward him. Swallowing down the rest of his anger, Pester held his palms up and said quickly, "I meant no disrespect."

"Why am I dilly dallying with you, anyway? I've never found much value in your filthy hide. Why do I get the distinct sense you've just been fiddling around with me and don't actually know where we're going?" Vex demanded, his tone dangerous. Extending a clawed hand toward Pester, he said, "Tell me, what would I lose by killing you right now?"

"A bit of your magic, for one," Pester gasped. "You've already agreed to my services. So far, I've proven faithful. Killing me in the middle of our spoken contract would leave a permanent mark on your skin, and you'd find certain spells would no longer work for you."

Pulling back his hand with a snarl, Vex whipped his head around and spied a bat flitting between trees. Screaming a curse, he shot lightening from his palm and fried the bat mid-flight. It fell to the ground with a dull thud. Pester cringed as static and the smell of burnt fur and skin wafted past.

Turning back to face Pester, Vex appeared to grow larger. "Find them," he snarled.

Shaken, Pester hastily pressed his ear against the tree trunk. A moment later, his eyes brightened as he said in relief, "The children! They've turned eastward a bit. Th that way."

Nervously, Pester flew over the dead bat with Vex trailing just behind him. Less than a hundred yards into their flight, a sudden chill cut through them like a knife. Pester's relief was replaced with dread. The wave of cold could only mean one thing—Lord Accuse was on his way. It was all too much for the young imp. *Nia,* he lamented, *I should have just let you die.*

Vex seized Pester by the scruff of his neck. "Finally, some relief!" he laughed. "I look forward to the look on your face when Accuse makes you into imp fritters."

Pester responded with a small, frightened squeak. The chill in the air deepened. His heart pounded in his throat. Then, with startling abruptness, Lord Accuse and his lackies, Prattle and Ire, appeared in front of them, the residue of an invisibility spell falling in sparks from their skin. Vex sneered and released his captive. Pester dropped like a stone to the lord's feet and laid as one dead.

"My Lord Accuse," said Vex pleasantly, "how good it is to see you."

The imp lord's eyes bore into the back of Pester's head. Pester expected him to strike at any moment. His whole body went rigid in anticipation. Instead, Lord Accuse said, "I'd say the same to you, Vex, but what is this I hear about you being the cause of a loose sprite and the deaths of nearly fifty town imps?"

"M-my lord," Vex stammered, "it wasn't my fault. Blame Pester here. He's the one who freed the Starbeam the sprite belonged to. If it wasn't for him, I'd still be in control of the situation."

Pester recoiled as Lord Accuse's gaze returned to him. "Is this true?" he demanded.

Somehow, Pester knew that lying or augmenting the truth would only worsen his situation. Perhaps if he spoke truly, Lord Accuse would grant him a more merciful execution. "M-my lord, my drudge was sick," he shuddered. "The Starbeam had brought a plague into town. Vex wouldn't heal her, so I sought the sprite and asked her to teach me a healing spell. Vex had bound her quite effectively to a post, but she was still able to show me how to do it, and—"

"You had her bound, but you didn't kill her?" Lord Accuse's tone was hard as ice.

"Sir," Vex cried, "she was completely harmless. She would have remained so if Pester hadn't stupidly used her spell to heal his drudge. Once healed, his drudge freed the Starbeam, who in turn freed the sprite. The blame lies with Pester alone. Don't you see that?"

"Vex, Vex, Vex. As an Original, I'm so disappointed in you," Lord Accuse sighed. "According to Addle, with whom I just spoke in Shades, it was you who led the town imps to capture her in the first place—an action that left seventeen maimed, thirteen permanently blind, and thirty-three dead. What Pester did is, in comparison, mere child's play."

Pester felt a sudden glimmer of hope. Could it be he might live through this?

"The sprite was dangerous!" Vex cried, eyes darting like a trapped animal. "Was I just supposed to let her escape?"

"You were supposed to go after her yourself, dimwit!" Lord Accuse thundered. At this, Vex fell to the ground, groveling beside Pester, who looked on in alarm. "You are responsible for the underlings you've been placed over—not Pester, not anyone else! The Shadelands stand or fall upon the actions of those who created her. Did you forget? You were a sprite once! Of all those town imps, you alone could have handled the sprite and gone unscathed. Would you have sacrificed all of Shades just to protect your precious hide?"

Vex whimpered. Lord Accuse turned his attention back to Pester. His icy gaze froze the young imp to his core. "On your feet, Pester," he commanded.

Pester pried himself from the ground, only to fall back to his knees. Lord Accuse motioned for Prattle to help him up. Supported by Prattle, his knees knocking together, Pester waited for Lord Accuse to pronounce his doom.

"Tell me, underling. Did you really cast a healing spell on your drudge?" The mildness in Lord Accuse's voice was unsettling.

"Y-yes, sir."

"And it actually worked?"

"Yes, sir," Pester replied. The air felt suddenly lighter, and the imp lord appeared impressed.

"Hmmm . . . interesting." Lord Accuse eyed the small imp. "Very well. Since you showed me proper respect and deference, and since you chose not to point fingers or deflect blame, I'm going to go easy on you." Pester's heart skipped in astonishment. He couldn't believe his luck. "I will grant you a full pardon if—and only if—you manage to kill this sprite for me in a timely manner. You have one week."

"K-kill the sprite, sir? Me?" Pester whimpered. His face fell. *How could this possibly be a pardon?* he wondered.

"You heard me," Lord Accuse spat. "As for you," he said, turning back to Vex, "I hereby sentence you to be Pester's servant, until he either perishes or so chooses to release you. You used underlings for your own advantage. Let's see how you like being the underling for a change."

"My lord, couldn't you just kill me?" Vex shuddered.

"I could, but what point would that get across?" Lord Accuse chuckled darkly. "Take this mark on your skin, underling. Kill Pester yourself or by means of treachery, and you'll wish you never hatched."

Rising from the moaning imp, Lord Accuse said to Pester, "Good luck with the sprite hunting. I'll be in the northern end of the farmlands for the next week taking care of another two dozen portals that have popped up from the Sunlands. Good evening, you two."

With that, he and his lackies vanished into the night.

CHAPTER 12

A strange calm came over Nia as she stared blankly into the gathering darkness. All hope of escaping the Shadelands was gone. The struggle was over. Nearby, Tanni had come to the same bitter conclusion. On his knees, he was covering his face with one hand and pounding the dirt with the other. Sobs erupted from his throat. Nia had no reason to cry like that. Tears were useless here.

Pulling her own knees to her chest, she welcomed the numbness that would ease any remaining pain. But the numbness would have to wait. Ease's soft voice interrupted its arrival. "Nia, please tell Tanni hope isn't lost yet."

Nia jerked her head up to search for the sprite. Failing to locate her, she asked dully, "Hope isn't lost? How? Can he make another portal?"

"No, but others can," replied Ease's faint voice. "Ask if he remembers Operation Lighthouse."

Nia looked back at Tanni, who'd collapsed facedown, sobbing despondently into the dirt. Seeing him like this, the same sense of detachment overcame her, leaving her with no desire to speak. *If I remain silent,* she thought, *perhaps this painful moment will pass, and I'll fade out of reality forever.* She imagined her imp finding her and returning her to the shack in Shades. Even that would be better than cowering under these watchful trees. She knew with grim certainty that were she recaptured Tanni would be too. Once back under impish control, his captor would make him blank just like the other Shadians.

A despairing moan from Tanni made Nia grimace. *Perhaps if he became blank it wouldn't be so bad after all*, she thought darkly.

Though nearly inaudible, Ease's desperate pleas grabbed Nia's attention. "Please," Ease called. "Nia, please! I can't hold on much longer. Ask him!"

Spurred from her impassiveness, Nia mustered all her willpower and finally asked Tanni the sprite's question. The effort was exhausting.

"Operation Lighthouse?" At its mention, Tanni's face brightened ever so slightly. He sat up, a ray of hope kindling in his skin. Wiping tears from his cheeks, he stared into the distance, momentarily lost in thought. Meanwhile, Nia sank back into numbness, glad of the deepening twilight and the ever-deepening silence. It was broken however, when Tanni abruptly cleared his throat. "Get up, Nia. Ease is right. We haven't run out of options yet."

Nia didn't respond. Instead, she answered by pulling her knees still tighter against her chest.

"Don't be like that," said Tanni. "Things could still turn out okay."

"Huh?" breathed Nia, doubtfully.

"I say that because of Operation Lighthouse. It's The Lumen's code name for the rescue brigade he sends out every month. They travel through the portals to save people in the Shadelands before they get caught by the imps. The rescuers are called Lightkeepers. I was being trained to eventually be one of them—that is, until I decided to strike out on my own," Tanni smiled ruefully.

"Okay," Nia muttered mechanically. Then following a brief

pause she muttered, "I don't understand how this has anything to do with us."

"Don't you see?" cried Tanni. "The Lightkeepers are probably in the Shadelands searching for me right at this very moment! If Ease can locate them and bring us to them, we'd be practically home free!"

"Ugh! How do you do it? How do you switch between joy and despair so quickly? It's exhausting to watch you," Nia sighed, focusing on the bush canes overhead to avoid eye contact with him.

"I do it because there are some things in life worth fighting for," said Tanni earnestly. Before Nia could escape his reach, Tanni grabbed her hand and tugged her out from under the bush they'd hidden behind. "Saving a life is worth fighting for. That life, Nia, is you."

Surprised, Nia stopped resisting and allowed him to pull her onto her feet. "You'd fight for my life?" she asked incredulously.

"Absolutely. Just like you fought for mine when we were in that run down old shack. My eye still hurts from where you elbowed me back into reality," Tanni grinned.

Nia stared at the faint bruise under Tanni's right eye. "That wasn't exactly what I'd intended when I went to save you," she said sheepishly. "Sorry for the trouble."

"Don't worry about it. Fiddi will wonder how I got it. I'll just tell him I got it from fighting off the imps," said Tanni. He swung at the air, fending off invisible foes, his exaggerated movements causing Nia to laugh. "Now that you've cheered up a bit, mind talking to Ease about where the Lightkeepers are? I'm exhausted, but I'd rather not hang around here until more imps come along in the middle of the night and throw us into this false portal."

"Are you sure these people would be willing to help me?" asked Nia, wrapping her arms about herself anxiously.

"Of course. Why wouldn't they?"

"Well, it's just that I've been here so long. They're looking for people who've just gotten here, and—well, I'm . . ." As Nia trailed off, she ran a hand across her ragged clothing and dirty skin. Compared to her, Tanni was a picture of clean. While his tunic was showing signs of wear, its color and original shape were still relatively intact. Most of Nia's clothing was mere rags that had come from dead Shadians her imp had told her to peel from their corpses. Would these rescuers accept her when she looked half dead herself?

"They'll help you, Nia," said Tanni encouragingly. "Ask Ease. I know she'll say the same thing."

Despite his and the sprite's reassurances, Nia did not feel convinced. "Fine," she sighed, struggling against the numbness that called to her. "Ease, do you happen to know where we can find these Lightkeepers?"

"Yes, I do. Follow me!" said Ease, sounding stronger than she had just minutes before. A dim light appeared in front of the children, floating between the shadowy trees.

***

Being an underling who'd unwittingly became master over an Original was hardly comforting. Pester never had delusions of grandeur before, and he didn't have them now—especially when it involved his worst enemy. Vex lay on his stomach, sulking and sputtering threats into the coal-dusted underbrush, his hideous form glistening with sweat in the pale moonlight. Pester had never loathed him more.

Despite being a former mine imp, Pester was remarkably well read. He'd devoured every scroll he could get his claws on in the more than thirty years he'd spent in the southern mines. Following his mother's death and his relocation to Shades, he'd scoured the town's literature as well. Unfortunately, not a single scroll mentioned how to deal with powerful, angry imp drudges who outmatched their new overlords. He wouldn't put it past Vex to sacrifice his own magic or life to kill his master if Pester proved too tyrannical. Nor did Pester doubt his servant would take advantage of him if he proved too lenient. This unprecedented situation would require all his cunning to make it work.

I can't set him free. He'd kill me in a heartbeat, Pester thought miserably. *But if I keep him as my servant indefinitely, I'll go mad.* With a deep breath, he said in a quiet, firm voice, "On your feet, Vex." The ancient imp didn't move. "I said, on your feet!"

Vex picked at his claws, unconcerned. "I'm sorry, did you say something? Your squeaky voice is too high pitched to understand."

"Keep this up," said Pester sternly, "and it won't turn out well for you."

"Oh?" Vex demanded, turning his venomous gaze upon Pester. Pester shifted uncomfortably. "How so?"

"You'd know better than I would. Wasn't it you who told me that imps who refused to obey their masters would experience a slow and painful decline, becoming mere shadows to haunt the Wanderer's Forest?"

"Who says I'm being disobedient? How can I disobey what I cannot hear?"

"You can hear me now. Selective hearing and dissent are remarkably similar."

At this, Vex shot to his feet, appearing eager to strangle his new overlord. Pester flinched and steeled himself for Vex's wrath. But a sudden spasm traveled up and down his servant's spine. Doubled over in submission, Vex hissed, "I'm up. What else do you want, my lo— What do you want, Pester?"

Swallowing hard, Pester said nervously, "I want help finding my drudge. No more watching me work while you plot my death. You're more than capable at location spells. Help me discover her whereabouts."

"What's in it for me?" panted Vex, another spasm forcing him to bow.

"Your own drudge," said Pester. Vex's ears pricked at the comment. "Find mine, and we'll find yours. You may not be an imp of your word, but I am. I made a deal with you that I'd get you into the mines if we found the children. I won't go back on that. The sooner we locate them, the sooner we can part ways. Got it?"

Vex spat and nodded, "Got it. Let's find those brats for you."

To Pester's relief, Vex joined him at a nearby tree. Working together, they cast a location spell.

CHAPTER 13

In the inky darkness, Nia noticed Ease's light was brightening and dimming constantly. The sprite's breathing was strained. She urged the children on well into the night, to the point of exhaustion and beyond. If they stopped to rest on a fallen log, she begged them to keep moving. It was well she did. The lullaby, which was once droning in the background, was growing louder. It unsettled Nia, but it was hardest on Tanni. He plugged his ears as he walked. But whenever he had to use his hands to push a low branch away or to climb over a fallen tree, his vision would blur. Once or twice, he nearly toppled over.

Sometime past midnight, Tanni tripped on a root and tumbled to the forest floor. When he didn't get back up again, Nia hurried over to check on him. He was sound asleep. Despite her own exhaustion, she shook him and called his name. It didn't work.

"You won't wake him," Ease moaned. "Tanni is a heavy sleeper—I should say, a *very* heavy sleeper."

Nia yawned, "You sound worn out yourself. Why don't you get some sleep?"

"Sprites sleep only on moonless nights," Ease panted softly. "Light is almost always enough to keep us energized."

"Ease, you're out of breath. Are you okay?" asked Nia anxiously. "Did I wear you out somehow?"

The shifting light landed on the ground next to Nia, her breath coming out in gasps. "No Nia," she wheezed, "you didn't wear me out. The imps did. I've been using my magic all day to keep your imp from finding us. It was relatively easy when it was just him. But another has joined him. I fear it's the imp that took Tanni and me captive on the night after Tanni tried to rescue you."

"If it was easy to keep out my imp, why can't you keep out this one too?"

"Because this is no ordinary imp," croaked Ease, her light dimming to a faint glow. "Eight hundred years ago he was a sprite just like me. I knew him well. His name was Soothe."

Nia sat bolt upright in the prickly pine needles and exclaimed, "Wait, you're eight hundred years old?"

"Two thousand, really—about as old as the lord of this land, and a hundred years older than Soothe. Still, I'm not the oldest sprite out there," said Ease, chuckling at Nia's astonishment. The sprite took several panting breaths before continuing, "So, as I said, we're being hunted by no ordinary imp."

"But, if this imp used to be a sprite, doesn't that mean all imps were sprites too?"

"No, not in the least," rasped Ease emphatically. "I see you're confused. Let me explain. Imps like yours came around long past the events that led to the birth of this mournful place. Your imp has tasted very little of the light. Most will never get the chance to. They were born imps. They'll likely die imps."

Ease paused for a moment to catch her breath. In the interim, Nia shifted over the crunchy pine needles into a more comfortable position. Her eyes felt very heavy.

At length, Ease continued, "Soothe and others like him were an entirely different case. They were born sprites. They knew what it was like to shine. Some were the brightest lights Spritedom has ever known. Yet," she said, "they chose to go against it."

"What?" cried Nia.

"There was a rebellion," Ease breathed sadly. "Long ago, a particularly powerful sprite, one who now calls himself Lord Accuse, led many down a dark path. I remember him then. He was the brightest light in the Sunlands. His name was Truth, and many—myself included—flocked to him for guidance. Until one day, pride consumed him, and he grew more and more jealous of the Starbeams."

"Jealous of the Starbeams?" Nia said, incredulous. Absently she had picked up two pine needles and was busily twisting them together. "But it sounds like he was immortal. Why would Truth be jealous of them?"

"Because your kind had kings. You do know what a king is, don't you?" The question hung in the air, while Ease once more caught her breath. At last, she continued, "Unlike Starbeams, the sprites had no royalty. They were all equals. But Truth wasn't satisfied with equality. Feeling underappreciated, he grew furious with the Starbeams, thinking their source of light came from the fey. From what I can tell, this thought ate away at his mind until he became obsessed. 'Why,' he reasoned, 'should I allow them to steal the light of my joy? Why not instead subject them to me so I can steal their joy?' So, he began poisoning their minds and feeding off their misery. That's when the Great Lie truly began.

"Through Truth's vast influence, a host of sprites joined him, and a rift formed in the Sunlands. A battle then took place between the fallen sprite's minions and the sprites in Sunburst, the great city of light. In the end, Truth and his followers were forced out of Sunburst and through the rift into the realm beyond. With the help of Starbeam kings, we sprites sealed the portals to that realm." Ease's breath slowed at this, and her voice lowered, "Perhaps foolishly we felt secure that the evil had been chased out and would never haunt the Sunlands again."

Nia frowned into the darkness. Dropping her entwined pine needles, she sighed, "Too bad they were wrong, or else I wouldn't be here. So, this is the realm beyond? Where exactly are we?"

"In a parallel world. In a realm the fallen sprites twisted in mockery of the Sunlands. It's called the Shadelands for a reason," Ease breathed heavily.

"Should have called them the Darklands," Nia scoffed.

"Some light remains here. If no light remained within him, Truth would be just like his minions of lesser birth. Hence, calling it the Darklands would be inaccurate."

A cool breeze rustled the trees and blew Nia's coal-crusted hair into her eyes. She brushed it aside irritably as she pondered Ease's comment. After a moment, she said quietly, "You said the sprites thought the Shadelands had been sealed off forever. Tell me how the portals reopened, trapping people like me inside."

"Of all sprites to fall, none was as grievous as that of Truth," Ease rasped mournfully. "He always was cunning and vastly intelligent. From what I can gather, he, and a handful of the brightest sprites he'd gathered to his side, began a great work utterly transforming this wretched place. I can only guess what source of energy they used to sustain themselves, but slowly the Shadelands came into its current distorted and grotesque shape, until nothing beautiful remained."

She took a few quick breaths and continued, "For five hundred years the Sunlands experienced peace and prosperity. Until one day, about three hundred years ago, the rift suddenly reopened and the fallen sprites, now transformed into imps, began luring Starbeams into their realm. They did it with enchantments the Starbeams could neither see nor feel. At first, no one could explain the strange disappearances. By the time my kindred figured it out, it was too late. The damage was done. The portals could no longer be permanently sealed, and several beloved Starbeams had already entered, never to be seen again."

Nia's cheeks burned in indignation. Balling her hands into fists, she asked, "What do you mean the portals could no longer be permanently sealed? If the sprites sealed this realm before, why don't they just seal it up again?"

"Would you really want them to?" The heartbreak in Ease's voice was unmistakable. "At what point would you tell them to do so—after you'd saved your own skin but left entire populations behind?"

Nia looked down, abashed. That would make her the ultimate nuisance. Imagine trapping every person she'd ever wandered past in this terrible place and leaving them hopeless of ever escaping. And here, she'd been afraid of simply stepping on their toes!

"It's not an easy choice to make," Ease said gently. "The Lumen wants to save every man, woman, and child who ever got stuck here, but Truth, now Lord Accuse, has filled this place with so many enchantments it is perilous for Starbeams, or sprites for that matter, to stay here. It's almost impossible to avoid succumbing to its darkness.

"Could the sprites launch an attack on this land?" Ease pondered, her glow barely visible. "Very likely, yes. But the imps have the advantage. They now outnumber us ten to one. More than half of our number would be wiped out before all was over, and the Sunlands cannot afford to lose so many of us. No, it's better to do what we can with our current services. Operation Lighthouse has saved hundreds of people. If we saved more, Lord Accuse would launch an all-out assault. Not knowing how that would end keeps us powerless to act more forcefully."

"I see," Nia sighed. "Then, why did you come here? Why did you follow Tanni into this place instead of staying behind where you'd be safe?"

Ease brightened slightly as she thought this over. "That is an interesting question. I tried stopping him, you know. However, as you're aware, he doesn't always hear me. Sometimes, I think he has selective hearing. He'd hatched out this plan a week before setting it into action. I tried getting The Lumen to stop him. But The Lumen said the boy would do whatever he'd set out to do. Blocking Tanni would likely lead to greater disaster. The Lumen advised me instead to stay behind and let the boy slip away. Slip away? As if I could!" Ease laughed, but her laugh turned into a wheeze. After a few short breaths, she continued, "I've been in Tanni's family for tens of generations. His mother and Fiddi weren't keen on my company, so it was Tanni or no one. Thus, on the day the boy snuck into The Lumen's office and looked up the spell to create the portal, I clung to him and made sure he wouldn't escape me."

"Didn't you think you'd die if you came here?" asked Nia, drowsily. Once more, her eyes felt very heavy.

"I knew I would," the sprite panted. "Nevertheless, I couldn't leave Tanni here alone. To his last conscious moment, I wanted him to know I'd be here with him. Until my dying breath, I'd never leave him—not even if I were facing Lord Accuse himself."

Nia smiled at Ease's courage and loyalty. But a moment later her head fell forward and she slipped unwittingly to sleep, dreaming of an army of sprites coming to her rescue.

CHAPTER 14

Dawn was approaching when Ease woke Nia in the sullen, forbidding forest. To the girl's surprise the lullaby had quieted down. At first, despite her grogginess, this made her feel almost cheerful—until she heard how utterly exhausted Ease sounded. Nia started to voice her alarm, but the sprite cut her off.

"Thank you for your concern, but that's the least of my worries right now. What I'm really anxious about is getting out of here. Oh, of all times for Tanni to be deaf to me! That boy will cost me dearly someday. Please Nia, wake him up. We need to get going, now!"

Even after a full night of rest, Tanni slept through Nia's attempts to awaken him. She gave him a hard shove. He groaned but slept on.

"He really is a heavy sleeper, isn't he?" Nia muttered.

Seeing a slow-moving, greasy stream nearby, she gathered some gray water in her cupped hands, returned to her friend, and dumped it on his face. Sputtering, Tanni awoke with a start. Snatching Nia's wrist in a vice grip, he sat bolt upright. His bulging eyes stared at her wildly, his skin clammy, and his body trembling.

"Tanni, it's just me," Nia cried. "Calm down!" She pulled at her hand but couldn't escape his grasp. "Tanni!"

In a flash of recognition, the boy smiled apologetically and let Nia go. "Sorry," he said sheepishly. "Nightmare."

"It's okay," Nia said, rubbing her wrist. "But if I spend much more time around you, I'll be covered in bruises."

Tanni reddened and apologized again.

Before Nia had time to reply, Ease whispered in her ear, "Enough words. We need to get moving. I'll heal your bruises later. But as things currently stand, we're mere steps ahead of the imps."

Nia relayed Ease's warning. Getting stiffly to his feet, Tanni pulled a stale loaf from his pack, broke it in half, and handed the half to Nia. In the stress of the situation she could barely taste it. While Tanni slipped his pack over his shoulder, she caught sight of a frayed pinecone dangling midair. Alone and exposed to the elements, the cone appeared to be hanging by a thread from a weathered tree branch. With Ease's faint light trail leading her away from their makeshift camp, Nia shook her head. This was no time to ponder something so seemingly insignificant.

*∗∗∗

Lord Accuse ignored his lackies' quizzical looks and flew on. He'd shot past the northern farmlands and was approaching the northeastern mines at the foot of the Sawtooth Mountains. Grim Pass was mere miles ahead, but the forest blocked it from view.

Coming across an abrupt clearing in the woods, an abandoned cart from Sunburst caught his eye. Lord Accuse stopped mid-flight to study the cart, his eyes glittering. Prattle and Ire stared from the cart to their lord, scratching their heads and whispering to one another. Finally, Prattle cleared her throat.

"Yes, Prattle?" asked Lord Accuse, stiffening.

"Well, my Lord, I assume there's a reason we didn't go to the farmlands?" she asked in a grating voice.

"Yes, a very good reason," said Lord Accuse impatiently.

"And, well," she screeched, "I assume you've also got a good reason to be looking at this cart?"

Lord Accuse crossed his arms, "Uh-huh."

"So—do you mind telling us what you're planning, sir?"

Lord Accuse motioned Ire to him. "Feel up to some enchantment magic, my friend?" he asked with a devilish grin.

Ire straightened at the request, "Your wish is my command, sir!"

"That's what I like to hear. Get Squeaky over here to summon some flour sacks for you. It's your job to conjure up some fruits and dried meats to fill the sacks. I'll fill the cart's empty basket with loaves of bread," he chuckled darkly. "Sets of fresh clothes and sandals would probably also be enticing."

"But, why, my Lord?" Prattle stammered. "I don't understand."

"I didn't figure your empty little dunder of a head would. Get to work," Lord Accuse snarled, "unless you wish to find yourself disgraced and out of employment."

Prattle rushed to the cart with a frightened screech. Quickly, she busied herself making the sacks, while Ire summoned a feast. *That's more like it*, thought Lord Accuse. Soon, the cart mirrored the merchant wagons he had seen in Sunburst hundreds of years ago. It overflowed with sacks of fresh fruits, colorful tunics and footwear, soft breads, dried fish, and salted pork.

Lord Accuse's dark eyes gleamed. "Nicely done," he grinned. "Now, make it look ransacked. It would look awfully suspicious unsullied, don't you think?"

His minions sniggered in sudden understanding. While they smashed the cart and its contents, Accuse flew to the tree line flanking the clearing. There, he reduced the ridiculous lullaby to a hum. It irked him to admit, but Pester did this right. The song he cast was powerful and curiously effective. Its enchanting influence seemed universal. Could it work on all Starbeams, though?

When Lord Accuse returned to his lackies, the cart and clearing looked like a tornado had blown through. He crossed his arms and nodded proudly. This would do. Turning to Prattle, he said, "Deception magic's one of your specialties. You know about Operation Lighthouse, I assume?"

"Yes, sir," she said cautiously.

"Can you imitate their signal?" asked Lord Accuse.

"I believe so, sir," she said.

"Show me, then."

Prattle bit her lip. Trembling, she lifted her hand and let out a pulse of energy that appeared to be the same frequency as that of the Lightkeepers.

"That'll work," Lord Accuse said. "Emit that pulse when I ask. Do it without useless questions, and you may just find yourself in my good graces again."

Prattle drew her lips into a fine line and nodded.

"Sir," said Ire, "there's usually more than one Lightkeeper looking for wanderers. Would it not seem strange if only one signal went out?"

"Excellent point. Three Lightkeepers should be sufficient," Lord Accuse replied. "Now, to talk with the mine imps, and then head to Grim Pass. There's work yet to be done."

The three of them took to the air in the direction of the mines, a dark purpose to fulfill.

CHAPTER 15

Pester grinned. Vex's eyes glittered. Throughout the night they'd labored to find the children. Now, with dawn fast approaching, they were zeroing in on their target. At times, their quest had felt like they were chasing a wild bat, but the sprite's concealment magic was weakening by their constant search.

"Hmm," Pester said, pushing away from a tree. "Odd direction she's taking."

"She's heading for the northeastern mines," Vex exhaled. "I would have expected her to steer clear of chokeholds or dead ends. Surely, she can sense them. She can't be that dense."

"Something must be drawing her that way," Pester said, thinking, *Perhaps Lord Accuse is tricking her.*

Vex wiped his brow and said irritably, "Operation Lighthouse. I can feel their pulse."

"Come again?" asked Pester.

"Must I explain everything?" Vex rolled his eyes.

"Yes," said Pester. "As my servant, yes—you must."

A growl rumbled in Vex's throat, "If you weren't the one in charge, I'd fry you for being so stupid."

"And yet," Pester said sternly, "I am in charge. What is

Operation Lighthouse? I order you to tell me."

Snarling, Vex raked a clawed hand down the trunk of the tree, leaving deep gashes. Turning back to Pester, he snapped, "They're Starbeam rescuers. Got it?"

"Oh," said Pester. He'd heard of the Lightkeepers, but not of their rescue brigade. "Well, this is troubling."

"You think?" exclaimed Vex in annoyance.

"We've got to pick up the pace and head them off. I'm not gonna miss this. Let's get going."

Vex spat, then followed without a word.

If I don't get this right, I'm dead, thought Pester grimly. He found it odd that Operation Lighthouse would appear so close to the mines. Most were very careful about where they opened portals into the Shadelands. The whole thing savored of Lord Accuse's work, as if he were trying to keep Pester from failing. *But when I catch up to the children*, he wondered, *how will I deal with that sprite?* With that disturbing thought, he led the way, hoping he was right about the imp lord. Otherwise, he and Vex would be hard pressed to find the sprite and children before the Lightkeepers got to them first.

***

Nia and Tanni were long out of breath. Still, Ease kept them at a relentless pace, only halting when they needed a sulfurous drink from the cloudy stream. Nia's lungs burned and her sides and legs ached. Her bare feet were bloody from tripping over stones. She was parched and lightheaded. Jogging alongside her, Tanni looked only slightly less worse for wear. He at least had shoes, though his sandals were starting to fall apart.

The sun was directly above the trees. Beneath the thick, dimly lit canopy it was hot and humid. Overpowered by heat and exhaustion, Nia fainted. She came to as Tanni was flipping her onto her back, his expression grim behind dripping sweat. The boy hovered over her anxiously, gasping for air.

"I can't hear you, Ease, but I know you can hear me," he said through tempered rage. "We can't go on like this." With that, Tanni collapsed onto his back, his chest heaving.

The forest and sky spun above Nia. Her skin was cold and clammy. Turning onto her side, she vomited into the needle-covered dirt. Searing pain wracked her skull.

"I'm so sorry," Ease said, her tone a mixture of remorse and fear. "My magic is almost worn out, but what use would concealment be if I ran you both to death?"

Trembling, Nia felt the sprite's small hand touch her damp forehead. For a moment, the throbbing in her head eased. "C-can you please let the imp find me? I just want to stop feeling for a bit," said Nia, her throat dry and scratchy.

"No," Ease said, "I'm not losing you. Tell Tanni to think of happy memories. I'll try restoring you both. After that, I'm casting something the sprites call wingfoot. You'll be able to run without tiring for a while."

After Nia relayed Ease's request, Tanni forced himself up. Closing his eyes, slowly a smile spread across his sweaty face and his faint light brightened until he glowed like an alien moon. Ease again touched Nia's forehead, sending a warm pulse through the girl's body. As the warmth radiated through Nia, it removed all her exhaustion, dizziness, nausea, pain, and soreness. She sighed in relief.

Ease groaned, "Now the wingfoot."

A second pulse traveled through Nia. In an instant, she was on her feet, hopping from one foot to the other, consumed with a sudden desire to run.

Next, Ease's faint form moved to Tanni. As Nia ran in place, the fatigue and bruises left Tanni's face. His light brightened, almost matching its original brilliance. Then, he, too, sprang to his feet and looked quite prepared to run a marathon.

"Wow!" laughed Tanni. "Ease—why didn't you cast this before? I feel incredible!"

"You may feel incredible, but I've never felt more drained," said Ease. "If I don't take a nap now, I may never recover."

"You've helped us beyond what anyone would have asked for," Nia said. "How can I help you?"

The sprite landed on Nia's shoulder and clung feebly to her dirty hair. "Run," she replied, her small voice filled with fear. "Just run!"

Nia froze. Her legs suddenly felt glued in place. "Why, Ease?" she wondered nervously. "What are you so afraid of?"

"No time for questions," said the sprite feebly. "Look, I wish I could say things will be easier now that you both are restored, but I fear everything is about to get a whole lot worse."

"Things are going to get worse?" cried Nia. Tanni, hearing only Nia's part of the conversation, looked on in alarm. "How so, Ease? What's going on?"

"Dear ones," Ease began, "I haven't just been concealing the three of us from the imps. I've also been using suppression magic to keep the lullaby at bay, and I cannot do it any longer. I nearly emptied my entire energy store on the two of you. I'm using the last bit now to keep the lullaby silent, so I can warn you before I faint. Once I do, the music will blast in your ears louder than ever before. When it does, it will numb your senses and dull your minds until you can't think straight."

"Ease, no!" Nia shouted. "If you faint, how will we escape the imps?"

Hearing this, Tanni gasped.

"I already told you," Ease said. "Run! If it's the only thing you remember ever doing in your entire existence, keep running. Your life depends on it."

Terrified, Nia turned to Tanni and shrieked, "Tanni! Run!"

The two of them took off as best they could in a north-easterly direction. Tangled in Nia's hair, the sprite grew fainter and fainter. "Run," she whispered a final time. A moment of eerie silence followed. Then, music erupted around the children. Nia's vision and mind instantly clouded. Her thoughts came slowly, as if through a sluggish soup. She repeated the word *run* over and over in her brain, but now she couldn't remember why it mattered.

Blindly flailing her arms, she felt something flailing back against her. To her left, she saw a boy running, his expression completely blank. *What an odd world this is*, she thought. *I wonder why it matters that we're running. Ah yes, we're both runners. We were created to run.*

Grabbing for the boy's hand, a slow thought came to Nia's mind. She knew him. His name was Tanni. They had to run together. They mustn't stop for anything. But why would they stop?

It seemed she ran and struggled for answers for an eternity. She knew an explanation was attainable if only she struggled long enough. But despite her best efforts, nothing made sense. So, she and Tanni continued onward, his gaze hollow, face free of expression.

Finally, after what seemed several lifetimes, it came to her—*Ease!* Nia thought in relief. *I must run for Ease. I must not get caught so the sprite can rest and recover. But what's trying to catch me?* She screwed up her face as she ran. *Oh yes, an imp. If it finds me, I won't get to meet my younger sister. I won't get to see my parents again. I can't let that happen. I'm never going back to that imp again. I'll die first.*

Nia kept a firm hold on Tanni. The pair began running impossibly fast. If necessary, they would run to the moon to find freedom and an escape from this horrible, twisted land.

CHAPTER 16

The chase was on. But the children were getting farther away, not closer. Initially, Pester was filled with hope. He'd sensed his song had finally overcome the sprite, and relished Vex's grunt of approval. That joy quickly turned to dread. From what he could tell, the children had gone from a jog to a blistering sprint.

"Wingfoot. Brilliant. Of all spells!" Vex hissed. His claws dug into the palms of his hands in fury. "If we don't do a similar spell ourselves, we'll never catch them."

"Do you have a similar one?" Pester wondered.

Vex growled, "Do I look like Lord Accuse to you?"

"Far from it. Will this do?" asked Pester, casting jetflight first on himself, then on Vex. Vex stared, open-mouthed. Though drained from the spell, Pester felt the full force of the ancient imp's compliment. He shrugged nonchalantly, "It helps to read a lot."

In annoyance, Vex snarled, "Know-it-all," and shot off. Pester quickly caught up with him.

Shadowy trees zipped by, while Pester's song ricocheted through the forest. As they sped along, a wandering Starbeam woman came into view standing stunned and completely overcome by the lullaby. Moving at such speed, she was only a quick blur of black hair to the passing imps.

Lord Accuse had a rule regarding wanderers. Any Starbeam found unescorted by an imp and deemed too old or unfit for service was to be killed—immediately. Pester had never run into someone fitting that description. He didn't relish finding one now. Glancing askance at Vex, he saw his servant deliberating the same rule.

"Thoughts?" Pester shouted over the whistling wind.

"We don't have time to go back and look at her," Vex yelled back. "Besides, she looked young and fit to me!"

Pester didn't look back. By following his servant's report he wasn't breaking any rules. Besides, the idea of killing a Starbeam made his stomach churn. Focusing on his goal, he swerved around the trees that came at lightning speed.

Unfortunately, maintaining focus wasn't so easy. The black blur of hair wasn't the only wanderer along their path. Four others came at regular intervals. At each sighting, Pester held his breath and looked at Vex. Each time, all was well. The wanderer was not deserving of death. Then, the pair rounded the bole of a particularly large tree. At its foot was a bent man with silver hair.

Pester's heart sank. *I'll say nothing*, he thought desperately. *I'll will the Starbeam to be a mirage or some kind of phantom.*

To his dismay, it wasn't. Vex came to an abrupt halt. Cursing, Pester followed suit.

"We're short on time," Pester said. "Is this necessary?"

"Oh, we have time," Vex said darkly, taking in the sunken eyes and sallow cheekbones of this man. The elderly Starbeam appeared lost to the music in his ears, his expression vacant.

"I don't believe I've ever seen one so old or so bent," said Pester, marveling at the gnarled features of the creature.

"Shows you aren't an Original. I've seen far older," Vex sneered, his eyes glittering with malice. "Put him out of his misery, Pester."

Pester crossed his arms and spat, "You seem keen on killing the old man. So, you do it."

"What?" Vex threw back his head and laughed, "Is little Pester too soft to kill a Starbeam?"

"No, just reminding you who gives orders around here. You just tried ordering me. Thus, the lot falls on you. As your master, I order you to kill the man."

Snarling, Vex turned and poured out his full magical wrath on the poor, unwitting gentleman. Pester heard the imp breathing his name with each evil blast. Agonized screams filled the air as the man, awakening from his trance, fell to his knees and begged for mercy.

Sweat started to bead on Pester's forehead. Bile rose in his throat. "Stop!" he shouted. "Vex, stop!"

Vex didn't. With each tortuous blast, he crowed in increasing glee and delight at the man's gurgled screams and excruciated shrieks. Pester shouted at him again and again but Vex completely ignored him.

Watching this horror scene unfold, something finally snapped inside Pester. Raising an arm, he took aim and shot out a killing spell. Instantly, the old man's body went limp, his face still twisted in anguish. Robbed of his fun, Vex turned to glare at Pester.

"We don't have time for this!" Pester breathed furiously, blood throbbing in his temples. "I asked you to kill him, not torture him. One more act of disobedience, and the deep magic of this place will make sure you thoroughly regret it. Besides, did you forget? The children are getting away!"

Eyes flashing, Vex drew to his full height and towered over Pester. Glaring down his nose, he spat on Pester's cheek. Then, uttering a curse, he shot off to rejoin the children's trail. Pester glanced at the man's mangled body in revulsion. In that moment, he truly hated being an imp. Leaving the ravaged corpse behind, Pester caught up with his servant, too disgusted to look at him.

SHADELANDS

***

Nia ran alongside her unresponsive friend until they reached an abrupt clearing. Almost immediately, the lullaby quieted down. Her sluggish brain quickened, and life returned to Tanni's expressionless face. She and Tanni looked at each other in relief. It was late afternoon. They'd been running for almost four hours. The wingfoot spell had kept them going, but it was starting to wane. They were out of breath and their stomachs gnawed at them.

"Where are we?" Nia asked, peering past the menacing trees into the clearing.

"Does it matter?" Tanni yawned. "Ease dulled the lullaby again. That's what matters."

"Are you sure she did it?" Nia wondered, glancing at her shoulder. "She's not talking to me." Ease's dull glow was just enough to show where the sprite lay unconscious, tangled in her hair.

"Maybe there's another sprite nearby," Tanni shrugged. "Come on. Let's get out of these infernal woods and see what's in this clearing."

Feeling strangely apprehensive, Nia followed Tanni to the clearing's edge, looked around, and gasped. Before her was abundance unlike anything she'd ever seen. Littering the clearing's grass-choked floor was a spectacular feast. Every fruit she had once known about and forgotten lay unspoiled in the weeds. The smell of fresh bread drifted in the air. She spied the tannish loaves spilling out of an overturned basket resting against a ransacked cart. Dried meats and fish, clothes, and sandals lay in piles in every direction. Choking back tears, Nia stood motionless, afraid the feast was a mirage—that it would vanish like the lullaby if she wasn't careful.

"Oh, Nia! Nia, we're saved!" Tanni cried gleefully. He stepped gingerly into the clearing, picked up a choice piece of fruit, and bit down. Closing his eyes in ecstasy, he allowed the excess juices to dribble freely down his chin. "These must be from the Upper Reachlands, south of Sunburst," he grinned opening his eyes again. They were starting to glow. "No one has finer fruit or wares. Come on, Nia. Pick one up and try it. It's delicious!"

Shaking off the lingering unease in the back of her mind, Nia stepped into this oasis of abundance. As she did, an inexplicable pinecone dropped on her head and rolled across the ground. Rubbing her scalp and staring at it in confusion, she muttered, "You don't belong here. How did you get here when the only trees around here are oaks?"

Suddenly, her chest tightened. A deep sense of foreboding flooded through her. "Tanni," she said shakily, "I—I don't like it here. There's something very wrong with this place."

"Are you insane?" Tanni laughed, snatching up a piece of salted pork and chewing on it ravenously. "Do you see me dying from being poisoned? Come on, Nia, eat!"

Nia's stomach growled. Years of gnawing, pinching starvation threatened to overpower her senses. Not wanting to disappoint her friend, she joined Tanni in gathering up fruit and cramming giant chunks of it into her cheeks. Tears poured from her eyes at the sheer deliciousness of it all. Throwing the last remaining caution to the wind, she took Tanni's pack from him, walked over to the scattered bread, and started replacing the old, stale loaves with as many fresh ones as she could cram in.

They'd only been eating a few minutes, but Tanni already looked remarkably better. He was radiating so much light Nia could barely stand to look at him. Flashing a grin, Tanni bounded to the fresh clothes, carelessly squishing fruits underfoot as he went. Digging eagerly through the clothing, he quickly rummaged through the entire pile.

"This is very finely woven cloth. Mother would approve." A moment later, he gave an exuberant crow and held up two large wads of colorful cloth. "I found tunics for us both!" Then, he was back in the pile, pawing through the sandals, almost beside himself with glee. "And footwear as well!" he called ecstatically.

Nia marveled at the new outfit Tanni gave her. She shivered at its softness. Never had she seen such a lovely blue on a piece of cloth. Retreating behind the wagon, she started to change. But just as she was pulling her old, ragged tunic over her head, Ease woke up. Prodded by Nia's undressing, the sprite struggled to untangle herself from the girl's filthy hair.

"Nia?" Ease cried, tugging against a matted lock. "What are you doing? What is all this?"

"Oh, hello, Ease," Nia said, pulling her old tunic back down and holding the new tunic out in front of her. "So glad you're awake again. There's nothing to be scared of. Look, I got new clothes!"

"What? No! Drop that thing this instant! Where's Tanni?" the sprite panted. "You need to get out of here!"

Nia let go of the long shirt and let it drop into her lap. Crestfallen, she asked, "What's wrong with the clothes we found? Don't they look nice?"

"Oh yes, child, too nice," Ease cried in exasperation. "Now, come on, Nia, snap out of it. Didn't you detect any danger here at all? Are you that senseless? That tunic would track your location no matter where you went. There'd be no place to hide if you wore it. Look around! Don't you think this place is too good to be true? It is. It's a trap set by Lord Accuse himself!"

"Tanni!" Nia shouted, her head starting to swim. "Tanni, where are you?"

"Over here," Tanni called. "Got your tunic on yet? I've got mine. Fits perfectly!"

"Tanni, I knew something was wrong with this place. It's a trap! Ease told me! Change into your old clothes. We have to go!" Nia yelled, scrambling to her feet. She jumped out from behind the wagon and met Tanni's confused gaze from across the clearing.

But at that moment, Ease screeched, "Oh no! They're here!"

Looking up, Nia saw the vague shadows of two imps come into the clearing. Terrified, she screamed. But before she could run, muscular Shadian men bounded out of the forest into the clearing on every side. Following the dark wills of the imps on their shoulders, the men closed in around them. A sudden, blinding flash rocketed from Nia's shoulder. The shadowy imp on the man nearest her disintegrated.

"Stop!" commanded a familiar voice. "Don't hurt the girl or the sprite. They both belong to me!"

Murmuring filled the air as one imp cried, "He's got a mine imp's accent. He's one of us."

"Yes, I am one of you," said Pester. "Do me a favor. Take the boy and Vex to the mines. Yes, Vex, I order you to go with them. I've got unfinished business here."

A furious snarl came from the shadow Nia assumed was Vex. "Release me first," he demanded.

"What? No. I've got no reason or desire to do so," Pester spat angrily.

"I hate you for this, Pester. May the full weight of every curse descend upon you!" Vex screamed.

"And upon you as well. Though something tells me my curses will carry more weight, courtesy of your continual disobedience. Now," Pester barked, "get going!"

The mine imps and drudges turned to exit the clearing. Vex, forced to go along, hissed and cursed as he went. Guided by the shadow on his shoulder, one drudge grabbed the shoulder of the now impless man and led him away with them.

Overcoming her shock, Nia struggled to run, but she found herself rooted to the spot. Across the clearing, Tanni screamed as the muscular drudges dragged him off. Ease moaned in grief, her voice nearly as feeble as before she fainted.

SHADELANDS

Nia watched Pester's shadowy form slowly approach her. Her eyes widened with fear. "Sleep," he commanded. A moment later, she saw no more.

CHAPTER 17

Pester stared wordlessly down at Ease, who had tumbled into the weeds next to Nia's head when the girl had fallen asleep. The sprite looked small and utterly powerless. He shook his head in disbelief and moved toward her. She scrambled away from him, only to back into the wheel of the cart. Pester grimaced at her fear. He knew the terror of being pursued, but he couldn't let her get away. Not again. Casting the same holding spell on Ease that he'd used on Nia, he approached the panting sprite.

"I never expected to find myself in a position where I'd be magically stronger than you. You must have gotten weak indeed," he mused, crouching down to look her in the eyes. They were frightened, but she put on a brave face and returned his gaze steadily.

"Does it feel good to gloat over me, Pester?" she asked, her voice startlingly calm.

"You caught my name there, did you? Guess it can't be helped. To be perfectly honest, it doesn't feel good. Not in the least," he said grimly.

The memory of the old man's shrieks echoed suddenly through his skull, and shuddering, he looked in revulsion at Ease's feet. Surprised, Ease searched his face. Feeling her scrutiny, Pester glared at her. The second their eyes met, she sucked in a breath and grief filled her lovely features.

"You've killed someone since the last time I saw you," she said mournfully. "But I don't understand. Your soul's not as black as it should be. If anything, it looks brighter."

Pester looked away, unable to keep her gaze. *I'm an imp. Killing someone doesn't bother me*, he thought angrily. But it did. He knew it did.

"Yes," he said at length, trembling. "Yes, I killed someone. It was the law. I had to uphold it. What's done is done."

"You say it's done, but I don't think you're fully done with it yet," said Ease, her voice gentle. "You're tortured by it. I can see it."

Pester scowled. Under her scrutinizing gaze his heart felt like it was being cut up into tiny slices and analyzed piece by excruciating piece. But he couldn't give in to this weakness. It would get him killed. "Well," he snarled, "what would you expect? Yes, I feel tortured. As tortured as that man was before I put a stop to Vex's fun."

"It was a mercy killing, then? That explains a lot," said Ease quietly.

Something burned within Pester. He dug through the recesses of his brain to pinpoint what, then wished he hadn't. *Pity*, he thought angrily. *She pities me. But I don't need pity. I need a place to hide. How dare she put me in this position. How dare she be too drained to fight back. I hate her. I hate her for entering the Shadelands with Tanni in the first place and taking Nia away from me. How dare she mess things up so badly and upend my whole world!*

Pester let out an anguished scream. Jumping to his feet, he raised a burning hand to sear her flesh. *I'll put out those pitying eyes!* he thought. *They'll never look at me again.* Focusing all his force and fury into the magic spell he was about to use on her, he reached for her face, his palm a mere inch from her skin—and froze. He heard Ease choke back a startled scream and watched her cower in terror. But he took no pride in it. He was a monster, just like Vex. Instantly, the hatred and fury drained out of him, leaving behind only deadness. Dropping his hand and hanging his head, he allowed the spell to burn out in his palm.

"I can't do it. I can't do it," he moaned.

Breathing heavily, Ease cautiously lifted her eyes to look at Pester. Aware he was being watched, Pester sat down with his back to her to deliberate his next steps. It would look strange to Lord Accuse that he hadn't tortured the sprite. *But perhaps*, he thought, *I could kill her quickly and quietly like the old man. No torture. No pain. Just a swift and gentle lights out. After all, Lord Accuse didn't demand me to give her an agonizing death. I just have to get rid of her.* The thought was greatly comforting.

Resolved, he slowly got back to his feet. Raising a trembling palm, he prepared the spell to strike–and stopped dead in his tracks.

"Oh no!" He gasped in anguish. "No, no, no! No, no, no, no, no!"

"What is it?" asked Ease, her soothing voice deeply irritating. "Is there any way I can help you?"

"By all darkness, by every curse! What was I thinking? What was wrong with me then?"

"Pester," Ease pleaded, "I can only help with what I know. Could you tell me what's bothering you?"

Pester struggled to compose himself. It took a minute or two to stop shaking. Finally, he crouched in front of Ease, his eyes staring at the grass nervously.

"You're a lot calmer than I'd be in your position," he said hoarsely. "Did you know Lord Accuse has burdened me with the task of killing you?"

A dead silence settled across the clearing. At length, Ease let out a long breath and said calmly, "If that is your task, what have you been waiting for? Just kill me and get it over with."

Pester met her gaze in astonishment. Staring at her grimly, he shook his head and said, "That's just it. You'd think I could do it easily. I am an imp, after all. But—"

"But what?" demanded Ease. Pester heard her heart hammering. "Why can't you do it?"

"Because I took an oath not to," he said tightly.

Ease let out a nervous laugh. Pursing her lips, she went silent for several seconds. At last, she said flatly, "How and when did that happen?"

Looking off into the trees, Pester allowed the memory to play in his head. "I was an impling, so you can hardly blame me," he shuddered. "Did you ever know of a sprite named, Trust?"

Ease's breath caught in her throat. She nodded.

"I had no part in this, mind you," said Pester, swallowing hard. "It took place in the southern mines just two months after I hatched. But I still remember it vividly. Trust was ambushed just outside my hovel. He'd gotten lost somehow while helping with the Lightkeepers. I can still hear his screams."

Ease choked back a sob. Pester tried to exult in her horror. Instead, he felt sick.

"I've never witnessed as much fury as was poured out against that sprite," he continued. "Yet, not once did he beg for mercy. Maybe he knew there wouldn't be any. Whatever the case, this only infuriated the mine imps more. Two straight days they tortured him. The walls echoed with his agonized shrieks. On the outside I snickered and sneered along with my two sisters. I didn't dare show what I truly felt."

"What did you truly feel?" asked Ease, her eyes glittering with tears.

"Pain," Pester admitted. "Pain and horror. The imp's motto is, 'Love darkness, hate whatever shines.' But I couldn't hate Trust for how he shined, no matter how much I wished to do so.

"By the second day, I couldn't take Trust's screams anymore. Quietly, I vowed I'd never be like those cruel adults around me. I'd never torture a sprite to death. Then, as his cries began haunting my dreams, I swore to go one step further. Never would I ever, under any circumstances, kill a sprite."

Once more the clearing went silent. Pester stared at the feet of his drudge, allowing Ease to quietly absorb what she'd just heard.

"You won't kill me," she said finally, "but Lord Accuse expects you to. What now?"

"Yes," Pester breathed, looking back at her, "what now? I don't relish Lord Accuse's wrath. He may give me a worse death than that of Trust. Yet, I won't go back on my oaths. I'll keep them till the day I die."

"That's very noble of you," Ease remarked.

Peter bristled, "I'm not noble, just careful. Keeping oaths prevents certain . . . consequences. As you've probably noticed, I'm not the largest imp in the Shadelands."

"No, but you're bigger than me," Ease offered.

"Sure, I'm bigger than most females," Pester frowned. "But among the males, I'm pretty small. So, I came up with a strategy. Most imps are unaware how the deeper magic works around here. I've studied it thoroughly. In the process, I discovered that broken promises and oaths lead to a loss of magic. Thus, by keeping my word, I could eventually outmatch the magic powers of some of the most powerful imps."

Ease raised an eyebrow, "Very clever."

"That's what I'm known for—my cleverness. But Lord Accuse doesn't know that. What Lord Accuse doesn't know can't hurt me. Besides, I believe I've thought up a way through this."

Standing up, Pester bent over the sprite to peer her over. He could practically smell her nervousness. "What are you doing, Pester?" she asked shakily.

Funny. Where's that brave façade she's always putting up? he wondered. "I'm studying your build. There's a certain spell I have in mind. Don't worry, I'm not going to hurt you."

Ease kept her head down and her eyes lowered. It certainly made his job easier. Being this close to her gave Pester an odd thrill. Conjuring up small measurements and placing them on different points on her body, he took a step back every now and then and studied his handiwork. One mistake and everyone, Lord Accuse especially, would notice.

Halfway through his work minutes later, Ease complained, "Must you keep me held while you do this? Wouldn't it be easier if you enlisted my help?"

Annoyed, Pester stopped for a moment to give her an icy glare. "The point," he hissed, "is to keep you still, so you don't mess up my measurements. Besides, you can't recharge this way or take off with Nia. I imagine you're plotting how to get her back from me. Not happening."

Ease bit back a retort. Pester returned to the markers and resumed placing them. After a painstakingly slow hour, he at last stood up stiffly, his body aching from the process. Taking in his work, he shrugged, "Well, here goes."

Emitting a grid from his palm over the points on Ease's small frame, his other hand hovered over the ground near where Nia lay asleep. A flash of red light erupted from it onto the grass. Straining to concentrate, he commanded Ease to hold still. Swallowing hard, she complied. Slowly, a perfect replica of her appeared on the ground next to Nia's head. Ease gasped.

"How did you just do that?" she asked.

"I used some mass from my earlier mercy killing and converted it into a duplicate of you. This way it'll feel and decay like your body would, were you actually dead."

The sprite gawked at her replica, which sat on the ground in the same position as herself. Turning toward it, Pester took aim. With cold efficiency, he blasted it once with a killing spell through the eyes, knocking it to the ground. Blood spurted from the wound. Ease flinched. Despite his fatigue, Pester chuckled at her discomfort. "Now," he said, "to disguise you. We can't have duplicates of you wandering around now, can we?"

When Pester was done, he was exhausted, but pleased. He'd accomplished everything he'd hoped for without overdrawing his magic store. His spell had rendered Ease's features nearly unrecognizable, but she remained beautiful.

Fixing her with a threatening stare, Pester said sternly, "Now, I warn you, Ease, stay away from Nia. I promised not to kill you. I didn't promise not to torture you or have others kill you on my behalf. Got it?"

Ease nodded, then said curiously, "You used my name. I've never mentioned it to you. How did you know it?"

"Simple," Pester said with a smirk. "I eavesdropped on your final conversation with my drudge. It's only fair to know yours if you know mine."

Cautiously, he removed the holding spell and braced himself. But the trickery he anticipated from the sprite never materialized. Instead, she gave a final backward glance before taking off through the forest canopy in the opposite direction of the mines. Breathing hard, Pester sent out a signal for Lord Accuse in every direction and fell tiredly beside Ease's fake corpse. With the real sprite gone, he felt a strange, dull ache in his chest.

CHAPTER 18

Nia woke to voices. But her ears didn't hear them. Like her conversations with Ease, these voices were perceived only in her mind. One voice—she could have sworn she'd heard it before—was deep like an organ. The air went cold whenever the creature spoke. The other voice was younger and had an air of poise and intelligence. It, too, was strikingly familiar. With grim certainty, she realized the voice belonged to Pester. She strained her mind to perceive the conversation.

"Not that I don't believe you. But I insist on studying the corpse thoroughly to be sure."

In spite of herself, Nia shivered in revulsion.

"By all means, my lord," said Pester calmly.

My lord'? Nia thought. *Oh no. He's talking to Lord Accuse!* Keeping perfectly still, she sensed the imp lord near her feet. His icy presence froze her to the bone. For a moment, she wondered if she was the corpse being studied. The thought confused her.

"Ease," Lord Accuse muttered. "I should have known."

A surge of panic rose in Nia's throat. *Ease? No! She can't be dead! Not after all the kind things she did for me. She deserved better than to die in the service of an utterly useless girl!*

"This is her body," Lord Accuse confirmed. "You aimed well with the killing spell. But I see no torture marks. Eager much to get it over with, Pester?"

At this, Nia boiled with rage. *How dare he be the one to cast the killing blow! How dare he leave me without a hope in the world!*

"She was greatly weakened by our combined magic, sir, but so was I. I felt too drained to use magic to prolong her death much further. I hope I didn't err?" said Pester, a touch of nervousness in his voice.

"No, no. You didn't err," Lord Accuse said thoughtfully. "You do look drained. Very well. Receive my full pardon. I assume Vex is still subject to you?"

"Yes, sir," said Pester. He sounded relieved.

"Good, good. You know, I could use someone like you in my service. Your lullaby has proven quite effective. Get rid of the girl, and I could have you work alongside Ire and Prattle."

Nia's heart froze in terror. The imp lord was trying to get Pester to kill her.

"M-my lord! That's very generous of you," Pester stammered. "But I'm afraid I can't accept it."

"Oh?" asked Lord Accuse, his tone surprised and disappointed.

"It's a great honor to be noticed by Your Excellence. I'm deeply flattered. But your servant has not the ability—nor the drive—to rub shoulders with the likes of Ire and Prattle. They are Originals. I am but a humble underling with no greater ambition than to quietly live out my days with a mine drudge among similar companions to myself. If in the future I find myself without mines or drudges, and should I attain greater capabilities than I currently possess, I'd most certainly reconsider your offer."

Nia's mind reeled. How could a murderer like Pester be so humble and reasonable? It didn't make sense.

"I can't argue with an underling wanting a simple life," Lord Accuse said regretfully. "Let me offer one piece of advice, though.

Don't bring your drudge to this mine up here. Bring her to your homeland in the south. You'll find better respect among your own kin. Find me when this brat has worn out her usefulness. I may still have a position for you when that time comes. Good-bye, Pester."

"Good-bye, and thank you, my lord," Pester replied gratefully.

The air warmed gradually, accompanied by the scents of bread and fruit littering the clearing floor. Released from her fear, Nia rolled onto her stomach and slammed her fist into the grass. Her heart seared with hatred and despair. In desperation she sought the familiar refuge that had always gotten her through difficult times. *Numbness. Yes, numbness will save me*, she thought bitterly. Slowly she withdrew, ready to become a mindless Shadian once and for all. But through her mind's thickening fog, she heard someone say, *Get up. Eat something.* It was Pester, speaking as if he still controlled her.

The fog lifted and was replaced by fury. Numbness had been the way she'd hid her faults, the way she'd avoided troubling anyone. That was the least of her worries now. With tears falling from her eyes like rain, she was determined to be the worst trouble Pester had ever seen.

"You get up! You eat something! Filthy little killer!" she snapped icily.

At first there was only silence. Then, Pester said in his most persuading manner, *There's no killer here. Eat and be refreshed.*

After years of conditioning, Nia almost obeyed. But she forced herself to think of Ease. The sprite was dead. Her murderer couldn't get away with it. Pester couldn't be allowed to act like nothing ever happened. This thought alone was enough to shatter the imp's manipulation spell.

"How dare you, Pester!" Nia screamed, jumping to her feet, and putting as much venom as she could into the phrase. Vaguely, she saw his shadowy form take to the air above her head and hover there. "Did it feel good killing her? Did it feel good ignoring her cries for mercy? You must be so satisfied with yourself. You've won. Bravo! If you had any decency left in your lightless soul, you'd do me a favor and kill me too!"

Above her head, she heard Pester panting.

"Well," Nia yelled, staring daggers at him, "what are you waiting for? If you think you're going to convince me to shut off my mind again and blindly follow you, you're mistaken. Go ahead, make me sleep! Use whatever magic spell you want. I'd still know the truth! So blast me like you did Ease, and who knows how many other helpless victims before her. You're nothing but a coward and a monster!"

"Stop," Pester pleaded, landing on the wagon top above Nia's head. "Just, stop."

"Don't tell me to stop! Ease–"

"Is alive!" cried Pester so firmly Nia was left momentarily speechless.

"Liar!" she said at last. "Lord Accuse saw her himself. What do you mean, she's alive?"

"What my lord saw was most certainly a dead body. But it wasn't her," said Pester, his voice tortured.

"So, you're a murderer and a trickster?" Nia demanded furiously. Her eyes searched the line of trees at the forest edge. "Where is Ease then? Who did you kill to make it look like her? Do you have Ease imprisoned somewhere?"

"Nia, please," Pester begged.

"Give me answers!"

"You have your answer. Ease is alive. So, be satisfied," said Pester, trying to deflect her from questioning him further. Unfortunately for him, Nia's resolve hardened.

"No. I command you now. Tell me! Where is Ease? Who did you kill? If you have any integrity at all, explain yourself," she seethed. Her irritation only grew fiercer as Pester started his lullaby.

"You've ended your—"

"Thoughts!" she snapped back. "Now your troubles sleep!"

A long pause followed. Nia kept her eyes defiantly on Pester's shadowy figure. At length, he spoke, his voice filled with anguish and grief.

"Stop calling me a murderer. Just stop! I beg you. I'm not a monster. I'm not a coward! Ease is free. I sent her off. You want to know how I pulled this off? You want to know whom I actually killed? Fine, I'll tell you. But for the sake of my pain, learn to hold your tongue before you have all the facts straight."

Pester went into a detailed account of the mercy killing. Nia listened in horror as he described Vex's prolonged torture of the old Starbeam man, torture which had only ended because Pester had put him out of his misery. Then, he described what took place between Ease and himself while Nia was asleep. He told about his childhood promise not to kill a sprite and how he'd used the mass from the mercy killing to form Ease's fake corpse before sending the real Ease off. By the time he finished he was exhausted, and Nia was in shock.

This isn't the cold-blooded monster I envisioned, she thought, her eyes tracing his shadowy form. *But I can't give in to him out of pity. Not when Ease is still out there. Not when Tanni still has to be rescued.*

"I forgive you for killing that old man," Nia said, drawing in deep breaths to calm her pounding heart. "I even forgive you for chasing Ease off. But I'm not giving in to you anymore. I'm taking back my mind. You can't touch it. It's mine." Pester said nothing. Taking a firm stance, she continued, "I know your name now. I know too much about you for you to control me. The only choice I see is for you to abandon me and go work with the imp lord. I'm pretty sure we'd both be happier that way."

"I—I can't," said Pester, his voice stunningly small.

Nia rolled her eyes, "And why can't you?"

"It's because I—I'm bound to you," he said hoarsely.

Nia sucked in a breath. This was not what she'd expected to hear. "What do you mean, you're bound to me?" she demanded.

"I made you a promise," Pester all but whispered.

"What?" Nia leaned forward. "You said you promised me something?"

"You don't remember? You don't remember what happened when I found you?"

"No," said Nia, intrigued. "Remind me."

Pester sighed. Clearing his throat, he said gruffly, "I found you crying alone in the Wanderer's Forest when you were five. Any other imp would have killed you because you seemed utterly worthless. But not me. Idiot that I was, I took pity on you. I figured with you being so sad your mind would be easy to conquer. I was wrong. You were and still are the most stubborn, aggravating, defiant Starbeam I have ever seen. It didn't help that your cleverness almost matched mine.

"I wrestled with your mind for weeks. I thought I'd be able to wear you down, but I was wrong. Finally, I asked if you'd trust me and follow my instructions in exchange for a promise. 'Yes,' you said, 'but only if I get to choose the promise.'"

Though Nia didn't remember the event, hearing about her childhood bravery made her smile.

"Believing it couldn't hurt," Pester continued, "I told you to name the promise. 'Promise to treat me as a father would his favored child,' you demanded. Like a fool, I agreed. I've regretted it almost every day since.

"So, like it or not, with that promise I have essentially made you my daughter. Since you're still an impling, I can't let you strike out on your own. Not while you're helpless. That would be breaking my promise. There are only two ways of getting around it."

"Which are?" Nia asked breathlessly.

"The first way, the one I'd recommend, is that you release me from my promise."

"No," Nia said immediately. "I won't do it. No way."

"Why?" Pester demanded.

Nia exhaled loudly and bit her lower lip. Considering her next words, she said carefully, "Because if you remain bound to me, you can't go around hurting others. Therefore, I hold you to your promise, and I promise to hold you to it as long as I live."

"Then there's no other option," said Pester in shock. "The only other way of getting around the promise is to kill me."

"What!" cried Nia in astonishment. "You're killable?"

"I am. Kill me and you'd be totally free. I'd no longer be a burden to you. All you have to do is knock me to the ground and crush my head with your foot. Have at it. I won't move, I swear," said Pester, his voice nearly emotionless.

Nia's heart began pounding in her ears. Rage overwhelmed her senses, and she took a step toward him. As promised, the imp didn't move. Disgusted by the pain he'd put her through, Nia raised her arm to backhand him. She imagined striking him so hard he'd fly right into the Sunlands. Finally, she'd have peace. She'd be rid of Pester and his lullaby once and for all. But as she was about to swing, an image of Ease's bright form flashed into her memory. Nia hesitated, her hand hovering in the air. The phrase, *Some light still remains here*, echoed through her mind.

Examining Pester with eyes which didn't feel quite like her own, Nia saw a faint glow at his core. Surprised, she reached tentatively toward him and touched his chest where the light glowed dully. Pester hissed. Despite his response and the clammy coldness of his skin, Nia's anger melted away by the light radiating faintly beneath her fingertips.

"What are you doing?" asked Pester nervously.

Nia chewed inside her cheek thoughtfully, "I'm noticing something about you. Something completely unexpected. Nothing you've done has ever darkened your soul."

Her natural vision returned and Pester's light disappeared. Taking in a calming breath, she continued, "You've done nothing to deserve death. No matter how long you've controlled me, no matter what you've done to me, you've kept your promise. You've treated me as a daughter as best you knew how. For that, I forgive you—for everything. And now, I make you one more promise. I promise I won't try to kill you again."

Suddenly, Pester's form appeared in front of her, as clearly as a Starbeam. He was small—slightly larger than a barn fowl—though his bat-like wings made him appear larger. His skin was gray, his features a startling mixture of ugliness and beauty, demonic and angelic. With his bald head and long, pointy ears, he looked very much like a gargoyle. Staring at her with cold, dark eyes, he did not look happy.

CHAPTER 19

Angry imps were not fun to be around. Overcome by Pester's furious expression, Nia turned away from him. She could feel his beady eyes boring into the back of her skull. Previously, she'd envied Tanni's ability to see imps. Now, she envied those who remained blind to them. The sight of Pester was the stuff of nightmares.

Stepping over crushed fruit away from the wagon Pester sat on, Nia collapsed beside a pile of salted pork and scattered bread. Eyeing it impassively, she reached out one slow hand after another and ate mindlessly. In her agitation, the food was practically tasteless. Her heart longed for Ease's mental clarity and comforting presence. But the sprite flew free somewhere, probably on the lookout for Lightkeepers. It wasn't likely Nia could locate her. And without her, the possibility of finding the Lightkeepers herself was slim.

She was reaching for more bread when suddenly and unbidden, the memory of Tanni's scream echoed through her mind. Hand hanging midair, she started to shake. Tanni was gone, and it was all her fault. Ease had been right to be angry with her. Nia had not heeded the warning of this place. In trying not to be a burden to

Tanni by agreeing the clearing was harmless, she'd instead caused him worse trouble by not continuing to sound the alarm. *Must everything I do hurt people?* She shuddered. *No wonder no one wants to be around me.*

Overcome with self-loathing, Nia bit down hard on her cheek. The brief jolt of pain sent another memory flashing through her. In her mind's eye, she watched herself accidentally knock the woman into the well in Shades. The memory was followed by a Shadian man standing over her, unleashing blow after painful blow. Reaching back, she rubbed below her shoulder blades, where scars remained from the man's ferocity. Pondering his cruelty, a tear of resentment trickled down her cheek.

Suddenly, it dawned on her. She wasn't beaten by a Shadian man. An imp using a Shadian had beaten her. She wasn't the source of Tanni's current trouble. The imps were mostly responsible. Besides, if she hadn't stopped to feast with Tanni, the two of them would have wandered into the arms of the imp-controlled Shadian captors and gotten thrown into the mines together.

"I'm still free," she said quietly. "At least in one sense. I'm not free of Pester, but I'm not stuck in the mines either. That means I can still erase some of the trouble I've caused Tanni by rescuing him. If I'm careful, maybe I can grab him and make a break for it like I did back in town."

"Pretty terrible idea, if you ask me," Pester said into her ear. Nia jumped. She hadn't realized the imp was on her shoulder.

"Get off me!" she snapped, pushing him into the bread pile.

"You didn't seem to mind me being there a second ago," he snarled, getting to his feet and dusting himself off. "Besides, have you tried thinking through the implications of what might happen if you were spotted trying to rescue Tanni?"

"I won't be spotted," Nia said stubbornly. "I'll just hide behind the houses and make sure I don't get locked inside one when I find him."

"Ugh! Do you even know what a mine is?" cried Pester, throwing his hands in the air. Rubbing the back of his naked scalp, he muttered, "Yeah, you'd be caught in under two minutes—tops."

"Glad to have your input on that," Nia said angrily. "Now, if you'll excuse me." With that, she was on her feet and heading in the direction Tanni had been taken.

"Where are you going?" shouted Pester. "You can't be serious. Stop! I said, stop!"

Suddenly he was in Nia's face, blocking her path.

"Out of my way, Pester!" Nia demanded, swinging at the imp. But he dodged her arm and flew higher. Burning with indignation, she marched on. She was nearing the opposite edge of the clearing when suddenly she couldn't take another step. Staring at her legs, she saw nothing holding her back.

"What have you done?" she shouted.

Pester, doubled over and panting, said hoarsely, "I've put a holding spell on you. For the time being, you're not going anywhere."

"You're a nasty little pest, aren't you?" scowled Nia. "You want to be rid of me. Why won't you let me go?"

Pester flew into view, his expression conflicted. He raised a hand and made a lowering gesture. As he did, Nia's body sank slowly to the ground until she was seated as his captive audience.

"Pursuing you has nearly drained me of my magic," he croaked. "Nia, you are so much more trouble than you're worth. Must you be such a nuisance?" Nia closed her eyes and started pulling in on herself. Pester sighed, "I meant that affectionately. I really did. With you being so headstrong, it almost feels like I'm scolding an actual impling.

"Listen," he continued. "The path you're trying to take won't work. It just won't. You're an intelligent girl, so let me explain. Mines are a series of tunnels underground. You know the coal dust you were breathing in back in the town of Shades? That coal likely came from here. Tanni was probably taken into one of the mine tunnels. The tunnels branch off in countless directions. Some are well lit, some are lit for a few bends, and some are not lit at all. Sometimes the lights burn out in random places, trapping your kind in pitch blackness. So essentially, going into a mine is like entering a maze. Let me be very clear: Go in without a guide, and there's no way you'll come back out again."

Nia's heart sank into her stomach. "But I have to try," she said weakly.

"Let me continue," Pester said. "Let's assume you're very good at directions, even underground. Great. But you have to get past the guards. Do you know why the mines are guarded?" Pester let the question hang in the air for a moment. When Nia didn't respond, he continued, "Sometimes southern mine imps try to steal the coal mined from the north. Reason is that their drudges aren't that great at mining, so they sneak into rival mines to snatch what they can to make up for the quota their drudge is lacking."

"What is a—drudge?" asked Nia innocently.

Looking away, Pester grimaced, "That's what imps call a captured Starbeam who's been made to labor for them for free. Yes, that makes you my drudge. I'm sorry. It's just the truth."

"It doesn't have to be. I'm not your drudge," Nia cried fiercely, "and I refuse to be so again."

"Fine," Pester frowned. "I won't call you that anymore. But as I was saying about the mines, they're guarded. Because of the amount of thievery that went on in the past, they're fortified at the entrance and at every station where coal is kept. So, even if you're very lucky and get in without detection, you'll still have to sneak past guards every twenty feet. It's hopeless, Nia. Tanni might as well be on the moon."

Though she'd told herself to be brave, Nia's courage deflated. Her stomach soured, and she wretched. Quickly, Pester released the holding spell, allowing Nia to double over and throw up into the grass. Breathing heavily, she curled into a ball.

"It's my fault. It's all my fault," she choked. "Oh Tanni, you should have never tried to rescue me. I'm so entirely worthless!"

For a couple minutes she lost herself to the pain. Pester wordlessly stared at her, the prickling of his gaze adding insult to injury. Nia wanted to escape, to get away from his eyes. She wanted everything to end. Getting onto her hands and knees, she spat into the grass to clear her mouth and started crawling toward the trees.

Behind her, Pester hissed in surprise, then came to land in front of her. "What are you doing?" he asked, confused.

"If I can't rescue Tanni, I'm going to join him," Nia said, spitting into the grass again. "Either that, or I'll ask them to kill me."

"No," said Pester flatly.

"What do you mean, no?" Nia demanded. Her voice felt scratchy.

"As your father by promise, I can't let you do that. I can't let you recklessly throw your life away. That wouldn't be treating you as a favored child."

"You want to treat me as a favored child?" Nia snapped, wiping her mouth with the back of her hand. "Then do so, for star's sake."

"Am I not?"

Nia glared at the imp and shouted, "No! Other than trapping me in this clearing, what else have you done recently to look after my best interest? I'm dying inside. The only friend I've made in years just got locked up in a hole in the ground. You've chased off the only source of comfort I've had since coming to this forsaken realm. You think you're acting like a good father? You've got a twisted sense of what a good father actually is. As your daughter, I demand you fulfill your promise to me as intended when I first worded it!"

Pester's eyes widened. Standing in shock, his hands dropped

to his side. A gulf of silence came between them. Finally, he whispered, "I can't do that. I don't even know how."

"Doesn't that mean you're breaking your promise?"

"Not in the sense I made the promise," he said firmly. "But as an impish father, I still must be held somewhat accountable. I've removed from you something you need. I must make amends for it. I cannot do anything about Tanni, but Ease may be able to help you there."

Nia's breath caught. One look and she knew Pester was in earnest. "Are you offering to help me find Ease?" *Can an imp be so kind?* she wondered.

"Yes, at least in part. I'm making you a—well, let's call it a deal," Pester said calmly. "Allow me to lead you to the Lightkeepers. I know their signal and how to follow it. Relax, Nia. I'm not plotting treachery here. When we find them, we'll likely find Ease. Once that happens, I'll ask Ease to take over as your guardian. As a father, that's the closest way I know how to treat you as you expect. In her care, I'll consider you in safe hands. Ease and the Lightkeepers can help you find Tanni, you'll all return to the Sunlands, and I'll be free to join Lord Accuse. Deal?"

Surprised by the simplicity of Pester's plan, Nia nodded. She got up and walked toward the cart where Tanni's discarded pack lay half full of bread and started shoving dried meat into the remaining space. Then, she stood up and looked expectantly at Pester, who'd come to land on the cart's rail.

"I'm ready whenever you are," she said firmly.

"Very well," he said. "Let's go."

CHAPTER 20

At the tree line on the clearing's edge, Pester paused. His mother's lullaby blasted through the forest a few feet ahead. The sound was comforting and nostalgic, soothing his agitated nerves. Just behind him, Nia stopped. Her mood shifted. Even before she spoke, Pester could feel it. She was angry.

"Turn it off," she demanded.

"There are nicer ways of addressing me, you know," he said sharply. Flying to a low beam on a nearby oak, he faced Nia. "You're a Starbeam. Didn't your mother ever teach you to be polite?"

Nia scowled and crossed her arms. A gentle wave of energy rippled from her body into his. Pester smiled and took a long, slow breath. He'd nearly overdrawn his magic store, but her negativity was helping him recover.

"Turn it off, please," said Nia, her pretty, dark eyes crackling.

"Not into lullabies?" asked Pester with a flicker of amusement.

"I'm not into *your* lullaby, if that's what you're asking. You said you wanted to go join Lord Accuse, right? But I won't move another step until you stop your nasty song from playing."

Pester rolled his eyes. For a moment, he felt as if he was talking to his sister, Taunt. She didn't like the lullaby either. But this wasn't his sister. It was his—whatever Nia was now.

"Fine," he muttered angrily. Flying to the bole of a large tree, Pester waved his clawed hand and cancelled his spell. The forest fell quiet. In the silence, he whispered an apology to his mother.

"Thank you," Nia said, her words like salt to his wound. "I've always hated that song."

Pester bristled. He knew why she hated the lullaby, but her words stung. After a few steadying breaths, he looked over his shoulder and said coldly, "Let's go."

The two moved silently through the dark, brooding forest. Pester welcomed the lack of conversation. It gave him time to calm down and reflect over the last few days. He'd gone from a nameless underling in the backwoods of Shades to master over an Original, killer of a Starbeam, near lacky of Lord Accuse, and now this: a Lightkeeper-seeking guide for a drudge he called, 'daughter'. *All I wanted was a quiet life with good companions and a good drudge*, he thought, bewildered. *What in Shades is going on?*

Two competing, rippling signals reached his ears. He'd sensed them for the last twenty minutes or so, but he'd been so preoccupied with his thoughts he'd paid them little heed. Now, ears pricked, he landed on the branch of a bush and listened.

Nia came alongside him. "What is it?" she asked.

Pester put a finger against his mouth and closed his eyes to concentrate. After a moment, he said quietly, "I think I finally sourced the signals from the Lightkeepers for you. Oddly, there appears to be two of them coming from different directions."

Nia leaned toward him. "Which one's closer?" she whispered hopefully.

To Pester's shock, a positive wave of her energy jolted through him. Bouncing around his insides, it addled his brain before finally absorbing into his core.

"Give me a moment of peace and I'll tell you," he snapped. *What of all curses was that?* Though unnerved, he returned his attention to the signals. After a moment, it dawned on him what was happening. "Ire and Prattle," he said darkly. "I'd bet my magic on it."

"What's going on?" asked Nia.

Looking back at her, Pester replied, "Yesterday, I wondered why Ease would lead you and Tanni toward the northeastern mines. I think I know why now. Lord Accuse wanted to attract Ease into a trap. Seems to have worked. He used his lackies Ire and Prattle to mimic the Lightkeepers' signal. You asked which signal was closer a moment ago. It's theirs. I can sense them just north of the mines in Grim Pass, a narrow road leading through the Sawtooth Mountains."

Through gritted teeth, Nia's breath hissed. Clenching her hands into fists, her face burned with anger. Pester flinched at the powerful jolt that surged through him. After a pause, she said hoarsely, "Do you know which direction the other signal is coming from? And can you tell whether it's a trap too?"

Shaking off another strange sensation, Pester cleared his throat and said evenly, "I can swear to you on every curse that the other signal is genuine. It's coming from the southwest, probably a good twenty miles from here. I can't cast wingfoot on you like Ease did, but I can help you avoid impish settlements and other places— places that could be as much a trap as the feast in the clearing."

"Why do you swear on every curse?" Nia asked curiously.

Pester laughed hollowly, "It's an impish expression. It's like swearing on something sacred, like stars."

"Oh," said Nia. "Well, I trust you, Pester. Lead the way."

Pester's heart skipped. No one had ever trusted him. Not even his parents. After all he'd put Nia through, why did she? Bewildered, he took to the air, leading in the direction of the real Lightkeepers. For the next hour, he was too stunned to speak.

Around midday, Nia begged Pester to stop so she could gather water from a nearby spring and get something to eat. Pester complied. Landing on a bed of pine needles, he waited for her to return from the brook. Soon, she was seated on the forest floor across from him and withdrawing provisions from Tanni's pack. In between bites of food, she realized she was the only one dining. "You don't eat?"

"Um, I do," said Pester uncomfortably. "But not from what you might call food."

"You don't eat food?" Nia asked. "What do you eat, then?"

Pester crossed his arms and shook his head. *If I told her, I'd jeopardize my hold on her forever*, he thought grimly. Fixing her with a glare, he snapped, "It's not for you to know, so stop bothering me."

At this, the girl lowered her gaze and stopped eating. She sniffled quietly. Another overpowering wave of her negativity poured into Pester's body, bouncing around and jarring his senses. His skin vibrated like a strange bell. Something wasn't right. The sensation reminded him of the emotional storm Nia had directed at him after she'd awakened in the clearing, as well as her attempts to rejoin Tanni. At the time, he'd thought the ferocity of her feelings would burst his skull. Somehow, even that was mute compared to this.

His head throbbing and his teeth chattering, he barked, "Just because I didn't want to share something with you doesn't mean I'm upset with you. Do you have to deflate every time I snap at you? Are you really that weak?"

Nia didn't speak. Instead, she sent wave after jolting wave of negativity into the imp, the power of her energy thundering through his brain and making him feel almost giddy. Fed up, he held out his palms and cried, "Enough! Think of something neutral—the pine needles or your tunic. I can't take your misery right now."

Blinking in surprise, Nia met Pester's gaze. The harsh energy diminished. "I don't understand," she said sheepishly.

"I don't either," said Pester, wracking his jostled brain to decipher the meaning of it all. When it hit him, he couldn't believe the simplicity. How had he never realized this before?

"Listen girl, you'll probably be angry to hear this, but you wondered a moment ago what I eat. Well, it's your unhappiness. It's anything that draws you down and steals away your joy. That feeds me."

Nia's mouth hung open. Color drained from her cheeks. The energy from her response was dull, so Pester continued, "The drudge I had before you was already depressed when I got to him. His emotions were muted and easy to handle. But you? You've always had more life in you. Because of this, your energy—both negative and positive—was amplified to the point of being physically painful. When I first found you, it aggravated me to no end. By the time I brought you into Shades, I was a mess. Then, I noticed the other imps had nearly lifeless drudges. Any emotions they'd had at one point was drained out of them, making them empty shells—void of emotion."

Nia shuddered, "How terrible!"

"I suppose it's terrible, but you once envied them," said Pester. Nia grimaced in recollection. "Look, I needed a way to dull you down and make it appear as if you were just like the other drudges. To my relief, I figured out a way to do it—my mother's lullaby. For several years it worked until, to my horror, you started growing immune to it."

"Immune?" cried Nia, her jaw dropping.

"Yes," Pester admitted. "You have no idea how aggravated I was the day Tanni showed up and my lullaby failed to keep you from noticing him. Only your sickness made you quiet again. But then you nearly died from it, and to keep from breaking my oath, I was forced to heal you and let your mind wake up entirely."

"You healed me?" asked Nia, astonishment written on her face.

"Again, I had to," said Pester, holding up his hands. "Look, I wasn't about to break my magic over a lost oath. The fact that it woke you up has been eating away at me ever since. But I've come to a strange realization. By deadening your senses, I was essentially starving myself at the same time and weakening us both. It's only now, with the lullaby stopped and nothing to lessen or filter your feelings, that I'm remembering just how much of a powerhouse you actually are."

Nia straightened up. With a wan smile she promised, "I'll try my best to dull my emotions while I'm around you. But as your favored child, can I ask you to be honest with me about a few things?"

"It depends on what those things are," said Pester defensively.

"Please don't be like that. What could be worse than telling me you use me as a food source?" Nia asked. Pester sighed. She had a point. "You say the lullaby was your mother's. Did she teach it to you?"

"She used to sing it to me," said Pester, looking off into the distance. An absent smile spread across his face. "She'd sing it whenever she wanted me to go to sleep."

"Does she still sing it now?"

Pester's smile disappeared. He shook his head and scowled.

"Why doesn't she?" asked Nia.

"Because she's dead," said Pester, glaring at her, his eyes daring her to push the conversation further.

Nia didn't look away. Holding his gaze, she said, "I'm sorry to hear that. How did she die?"

"You seriously can't take a hint, can you?" Pester snarled.

"I know you don't want to talk about it. But I can see it's a hurt that hasn't healed yet." Nia replied. "I'm just trying to help."

Pester looked away and once more saw the vision of his mother vanishing in a cloud of dust. Angrily, he got to his feet and went to lean against a tree. Nia remained silent, but her disappointment unsettled him. He wasn't sure what to do with this strange emotion.

"I'm sorry, Pester," Nia said quietly. She didn't try to approach him.

Kicking a pinecone, which sent a small forest creature scurrying away, Pester rubbed the wisps on his bald head. At length, he said thickly, "There was an accident."

"An accident?" Nia asked softly.

"Yes. A cave in. In other words, the mine my sisters and I were in with our drudges collapsed," said Pester. Nia gasped. Swallowing hard, his mind relived the scene. "The three of us raced with our drudges to get out of there, but it was too late. The rocks tumbled down around us, killing our drudges, and knocking us into the darkness. Before I lost consciousness, all I could think about was that I never did anything of true value.

"It wasn't long before my parents heard of the cave in. Mother was one of the Originals who'd come with Lord Accuse into the Shadelands. Her name was Lull. She flew to the collapsed tunnel with my father, and the two of them joined the other mine imps and their drudges, trying to dig us out. From what I'm told, she spent a lot of her magic trying to locate us. By the time Mother found us, we'd been in the collapsed tunnel for almost two days. In that time, not once had she left the site. She was completely exhausted. When we were unburied, we were almost dead. Even so, she refused to be dragged away by my father, who was afraid she'd overexert herself. The other imps pleaded with her to let us die. After all, without healing magic we'd never recover.

"My sisters and I were Mother's first and only hatching. She couldn't bear the idea of leaving us to our fate," Pester sighed, passing a hand over his eyes. If Nia could have fed off his pain, she'd be gorging herself right now. With a deep breath, he continued, "When Mother informed my father she was going to heal us, he tried to stop her. But when she remained adamant, he begged her to heal his daughters first. After all, he and I never saw eye to eye. Mother complied. By the time she got to me, she was so drained, my father begged her to forget about me. 'Let him pass,' he told her. 'He's not worth it.' But it was no use. Before he could stop her, Mother cast the last of her magic, and I awoke to watch her cry out to him before disintegrating into dust."

A long pause followed the end of Pester's story. Finally, Nia whispered, "I'm so, so sorry."

Pester nodded and stared into the trees. Soon, he realized Nia's sympathetic energy was feeding his emptiness and soothing his soul. It was new and strange. Never before had he gained energy from something that wasn't negative. Perhaps Lord Accuse had been wrong when he told the imps positivity would drain its victims. In the nest, his mother even told him sprites only grew weaker when Starbeams were full of joy.

"Thank you," Pester said, quietly.

"For what?" asked Nia.

"For teaching me something crucial. It's a lesson I probably won't ever forget," said Pester. Ignoring Nia's questions about his cryptic phrase, he wiped his mouth with the back of his hand and looked off into the gloomy forest. "Hurry up and gather your pack. We've got a long hike ahead of us."

Nia busied herself with collecting her things. A moment later, she jumped to her feet and slung her pack.

Impressed by her quickness, Pester gave her a curt nod, and said, "Ready? To the Lightkeepers, then."

Taking to the air, he led the way, eager to get the journey over with.

CHAPTER 21

Nia spent an uncomfortable night under the brooding gaze of the sinister forest. Dark shadows prowled the perimeter of her makeshift camp. Despite having spent a few nights beneath the canopy previously, this was her first without Ease's comforting light. The evening before, she'd slept under Pester's spell in the middle of the clearing. Although the imp didn't venture far from her all night, Nia felt utterly unprotected and exposed. She could have sworn the trees were whispering dark thoughts to each other overhead. By the time dawn's dull, gray light appeared, she was exhausted. Sitting up, she rubbed her back where a root had been sticking into it.

"You look awful," said Pester, landing on the ground beside her.

"So do you," Nia grunted, "but that can't be helped."

"Grumpy, I see," chuckled Pester. He sounded almost chipper. "Well, here's food for thought. After today's hike, we should reach the Lightkeepers. You'll be out of these woods in no time."

Nia frowned. She knew Pester was only happy because he was about to get rid of her. Somehow, the idea of losing him unsettled her. The imp was more a part of her than she'd realized. *Besides, didn't he heal me on my death bed?* she wondered, chewing thoughtfully on her cheek. As unbelievable as it sounded, that knowledge was slowly softening her hatred of him.

Reaching for her pack, she withdrew some provisions. The bread was becoming hard and crusty, but it was still edible. Nia gnawed on it until her jaw hurt. As she chewed, she felt the brooding trees grow more and more sinister. Finally, she couldn't ignore them any longer.

"I hate your forest," she told Pester. "How you stand it I can't imagine."

"You get used to it," said Pester, gazing at the trees with a frown.

"Sounds like you secretly don't like it much either," said Nia, swallowing the last bite of bread as she slung her pack across a shoulder. "Shall we get going then?"

"On the contrary, I find this place quite peaceful," Pester smirked. "Follow me."

According to her imp, Nia was roughly ten miles from her rescuers. It would be a long hike, but with any luck they'd reach them by midafternoon. Nia's feet were already sore. Her heels were bruised. Small cuts and scrapes burned whenever she waded through shallow streams or crossed areas of low-lying marsh. Unfortunately, the area they were currently in was one big wetland. Coupled with her restless night, she struggled to keep her thoughts neutral, even with Pester's frequent reminders.

"Try being a bit more cheerful, would you? My body is recharged already," he grumbled bitterly an hour into her trek. "I feel like if I feed anymore from the ocean of your misery I might explode."

It wasn't easy to be positive—not in a place like this. Still, Nia found the idea of an imp asking his Shadian to cheer up almost amusing. *Guess I could give it a try*, she thought with a frown. Focusing on her coming reunion with Ease, her spirits slowly rose. Pester grunted in approval and the two continued.

Around noon, Pester called Nia to a halt. "Eat something," he snarled, rubbing his temples. "Think only of chewing for a while, for pity's sake. Now there's too much positive energy coming out of you. If you have to think, keep it neutral."

"Sorry," said Nia sheepishly, sitting down to brush clay from the bottoms of her stinging feet. Suddenly, Pester gave a low, startled hiss. Nia looked up.

"By every curse, it can't be!" Pester cried, grabbing at his scalp in agitation. Peering into the distance, his eyes were wide as saucers. "Nia, I beg of you, please. Please pretend to be under my control for a few minutes. My sister, Wither is on the way."

The idea of even pretending to be under his control again was sickening. Nia reached toward her pack to nonchalantly rummage through it, and asked, "And why should I do that?"

In a moment, Pester was in front of her, hands clasped, eyes clouded with fear. "As your father, I beg of you. If ever I needed you to act like my favored child, now would be it. Please, for me, just go blank for a little while, okay? I don't want to make you go to sleep."

Nia stared hard at him. Clearing her throat, she said, "First, promise me you'll leave my mind forever under my own control."

"Nia, please," Pester pleaded.

"Promise me!" said Nia fiercely.

Shocked, Pester breathed the new oath. Satisfied, Nia just had time to clear her mind and stare blankly into the distance when Wither arrived.

Upon seeing her brother, Pester's sister hissed in surprise, "Well, this is unwanted and unexpected. I knew I sensed an imp here. But you? What in Shades are you doing here, brother?"

"I've just recaptured my drudge and was . . ." Pester trailed off, his eyes crossing slightly. Being called 'Pester's drudge' caused Nia's insides to burn. Her powerful emotions flared up, muddling his thoughts, and rendering him unable to speak. When the jolt of energy finally passed, Pester cleared his throat and said shakily, "What—what are you doing here, sister?"

Wither sneered, "My drudge is dead. I'm looking for another one." Suddenly, she tore into Nia's field of vision, fluttering just in front of her face. The creature's dark eyes pierced into the girl's. Nia struggled to remain unfocused. But in spite of herself, she couldn't help noticing the imp's gray skin matched her brother's. Despite looking very much like a gargoyle, she was distinctly feminine, almost pretty. "Stop the act," Wither demanded, putting her fists on her hips. "I know you can see me."

Pester gasped. Nia blinked. Her eyes came back into focus, and she swallowed hard. Tilting her head, she asked, "How could you tell?"

"Oh, come on, really? How couldn't I?" Wither turned her back on Nia and landed on a low branch. Then peering back slyly at the girl, she snorted, "You've got some temper in that young Starbeam head of yours. I'd bet you a thousand curses your irritation could be felt a mile away."

"It's—it's not what you think," stammered Pester, his eyes wide. In her head, Nia heard his voice mutter angrily, *I swore another oath for this?*

"Come off it, idiot. It's exactly what I think," Wither laughed. "So, you're headed in the direction of the Lightkeepers, are you? Care to explain yourself a bit? Wanting to join the slimy little glow worms in the land of sunshine and rainbows, brother?"

"How dare you!" Nia screamed.

To Nia's astonishment, Wither and Pester fell to the ground, writhing, covering their ears. Drawing back, she thought in surprise, *I did that! My emotions—they did that!* Her face burned with guilt.

"I don't like the way you talk about sprites, Wither," Nia said at length. "Do you have anything else to say? Or did you just come here to gloat?"

Panting, Wither got to her feet. Pester sat and stared at Nia. Crossing her arms, Wither looked from the girl to Pester. Then, she gave a little start. Eyeing her brother up and down, her eyes narrowed, and she said coldly, "Now I can see why you used mother's lullaby on her so much, Pester. She's quite the force, isn't she? Not that it's doing you too much good now. Look at you, you're glowing!"

Though the imp's light was faint, it was there, just perceptible to the naked eye. Pester yelped, "No! It can't be!"

"Well," said Wither, backing toward the forest, "I think I've seen enough."

Before she could take another step, Pester raised a palm toward his sister and cast a holding spell. Instantly, his face became drawn, and he hunched over.

Snarling, Wither said furiously, "What are you doing? Ugh! Let me go, you imbecile! You can't hold me forever!"

Pester wheezed and stared at his faintly glowing hands in horror. Looking back at his sister, he said hoarsely, "You're right, Wither, I can't hold you forever. But please hear me out. I didn't ask for this. As kin, I beg of you to reconsider what you're planning to do."

Wither grew quiet, her expression conflicted. The hold Pester had on her was weakening. Nia watched the situation unfold, feeling hopeless.

Then, to her astonishment, Ease's voice echoed in her head, saying, *This one carries light unseen.* Nia's vision changed with the words, and she saw a dull light at Wither's core.

"Wither," Nia said softly, "you hide your own light well. I'm impressed."

Wither's eyes widened. Then, Pester's spell broke. He dropped onto his face, his body glistening with sweat. "Please, sister," he panted into the dirt.

Crossing her arms and staring at Nia, Wither stood thinking

for a few moments before saying, "It pains me to admit this, but your eyes are extraordinary. To see what you've just seen takes an incredible gift. Clearly the sprite put more into you than just some kind of restoration spell. She must have far greater faith in you than I.

"I must admit," she continued, turning to Pester, "I'm hardly surprised to see your light. After all, brother, you came out fully glowing when you hatched."

"I what?" cried Pester tiredly, getting slowly to his knees.

"Oh, yes," Wither said. "Why do you think father hated you so much? Why do you think mother had to protect you in the nest? It wasn't because you were a runt, although you most certainly were. You were born a fully shining sprite. And you know what? I'll let you in on a little secret Nia just figured out. So was I."

Pester stood up beside his sister, his legs visibly shaking. Though substantially taller than Wither, he appeared smaller. "There's no way, Wither—no way you were born a sprite," he said, his voice trembling. "Taunt would have hated you just like she hated me."

Wither frowned, "I didn't glow very brightly, but I was indeed a sprite. Do you know why mother sang the lullaby to us so much? She was turning us into imps, brother. Why do you think the wording is so bizarre? Think about it. 'You've ended your thoughts, now your troubles sleep.' Our mother knew she had to fix us, or we'd be slaughtered by father or Taunt, or else by the entire mine encampment."

Pester turned several shades paler. Leaning heavily against a tree, he said thickly, "I never knew about the lullaby. This changes everything."

"It does, doesn't it? Listen, I'm gonna admit something to you, Pester. As much as I hate saying it, I never really hated you. I only ever hated Taunt. Living with her this whole time has been a nightmare."

The two of them looked at each other for a long moment. Pester smiled.

Turning away, Wither looked back at Nia, who was overwhelmed by the scene in front of her. The imp's dark eyes left Nia feeling cold and unnerved. They reminded her of black, bottomless wells.

"I've spent my life loathing your kind. Only two kinds of Starbeams have ever come my way: those who were lifeless, and those who were thieving the lifeless out from under my nose. But I'll admit," Wither said firmly, "something about you intrigues me. I was perfectly prepared to go straight to Lord Accuse to let him know you were escaping, but now I think I've decided against it."

Nia's heart began to pound. "You've—why?" she stammered.

"Good question. You are surprisingly clever for a drudge." Wither paced in front of Nia. "Let me tell you a bit about myself. I've had three drudges so far in my lifetime. Each one has been a complete disappointment to me. Now, my eyes are opened to see why. They were all dead inside. They had nothing further to give. By being around them, I became completely jaded. But witnessing the energy and power of a fully feeling, fully functioning child? That's something I don't think I'll ever forget. Somehow, you brought my brother back to his roots. If I'm not careful, you might bring me back to mine as well."

"Would you even want to be a sprite?" asked Nia.

"Maybe," Wither smiled wanly. "Sprites are powerful creatures. I could use a bit of that power right now."

"But imps can't become sprites," cried Pester. "Lord Accuse says it's impossible."

"Well, he's wrong. Look no further than yourself to see it. As for you," she said, turning back to Nia, "I'm going to take a chance on you. Pester may be surprised to hear this, but a small handful of imps in Shades have grown restless like me. One of them is Addle. Together, we've seen past the lies we've been fed all our lives. We're sick of the system we've got. We want change. Pester, here I am looking at this drudge of yours, and I can tell she has a big part to play in bringing about that change. I'll be curious to see how."

"I don't want to bother anybody," Nia said, staring at her feet.

"No?" Wither asked, lifting a brow. "Oh, but you will. Extraordinarily so. I'm anxious to see just how many are bothered by you. But that comes later. For starters, I have a task for you."

Settling on a nearby root, she smoothed her silver hair over her body like a garment and continued, "Vex left Shades without offering one healing spell to save the drudges that had been sickened by the plague going around. Two-thirds of them have died so far as a result, and the town is in disarray from the displaced imps looking for new wanderers to conquer. Just after Vex was driven out of town, I led my sick drudge into his path and confronted him, asking him to heal her. You know what he did instead? He took one look at her and shot out a killing curse at her! He told me I was better off for it before shooting off into the woods. Needless to say, I'm quite furious with Vex. I want revenge.

"Right now, in these very woods," said Wither angrily, gesturing widely at the trees, "he's out in pursuit of a drudge thief from the northeastern mines. The drudge he's trying to recover is the boy who tried rescuing you out of Shades, and with whom you ran off after your lucky escape."

Nia gasped. Pester's eyes widened. Regathering herself, Nia asked, "So your favor is what, to get Tanni back from Vex?"

"Precisely," said Wither with a toothy grin. "The imp who took Tanni was a fool to think he'd win against an Original in a magic duel. We all know Vex will totally destroy him. So, while he fights over Tanni, steal the boy, and make a break for it to the Sunlands. Oh, and after you're successful, come back to the Shadelands as one of the Lightkeepers."

"Why would—why would you want me to do that?" Nia questioned breathlessly.

"So you can wreak as much havoc on the Shadelands as one Starbeam can possibly manage," Wither chuckled darkly. "To be honest, I'm sick of how boring this place is."

"I'll do what I can," Nia said bravely. Even so, her heart sank.

"Good. You have three days to reach your friend. Lucky for you, the place is not that far. Pester will know how to find him," said Wither, giving her brother a knowing glance. "Tanni's being taken to the Battle Marsh."

"Where do you plan to go from here, Wither?" asked Pester.

"I suppose to aimlessly look for a drudge. I'm in no hurry, though," she said with a sigh. "Goodbye, brother."

"Goodbye," said Pester.

Giving a final look at Nia, Wither said sharply, "I'm counting on you." Then, she disappeared through the trees.

Nia looked at Pester expectantly and said, "You heard her, didn't you? To the marsh."

"No," said Pester firmly. "Whatever you do from here is on you. We go to Ease. I've had enough of this."

With a heavy heart, Nia hurried to keep up with Pester, who, in spite of his exhaustion, seemed determined to rid himself of his sprite-producing drudge as quickly as possible.

CHAPTER 22

Just beyond the crest of the hill in front of them, something big was happening. The air was icy cold, and booms and flashes of light rent the canopy of the trees. Nia froze. She knew that cold feeling. Lord Accuse was nearby. Pester halted, cursing under his breath.

"Great. Of all things to run into, this is the most unwelcome. And to think I usually would applaud my lord shutting the Starbeam portals." Turning to Nia, he said quietly, "Whatever you do, keep your emotions guarded. The Lightkeepers' fear may give you some concealment, but one angry or happy burst from you, and we're dead. Got it?"

"I'll do my best," Nia promised. "But what are you planning to do?"

"I'm going to go scout things out first. See that overhang against the hill to the right?" asked Pester, pointing. "Go beneath it and wait for me there. I shouldn't be gone long."

The overhang was partly hidden behind a curtain of dripping overgrowth. Nia used a stick to move aside cobwebs and crawled inside. The floor was wet, the air musky. Icy water dripped from the ceiling, slowly soaking her clothes and hair. She began to shiver. Remembering Pester's warning, she muted her agitation and took a seat. The clay floor's moisture seeped into her ragged clothing, making her even colder. Soon, her teeth chattered. All the while, the sound of the battle continued above her, intermixed with shouts from the Lightkeepers. She wondered if Ease was up there fighting Lord Accuse. Despite the cold, the thought made her smile.

When Pester returned, he was breathing hard, his face ashen. "Ten Lightkeepers are defending the portals," he said. "One portal seems unnoticed and unguarded, even by Lord Accuse and the twenty-odd imps who are with him. I'm going to bring you to it, and you're going to go through."

"Did you see Ease?" asked Nia.

"No, and I don't think she's in the Shadelands. I haven't sensed her for a day, though I'm certain we were on her trail. I have a strong suspicion she made it to the Sunlands already. So, the sooner you go through to that realm, the sooner the two of you can be reunited. On your feet," Pester said, grabbing at Nia's hand. "Let's go."

"What about Tanni?" asked Nia, swallowing her fear.

"What about him?" Pester asked tiredly. "Listen, this may be your only chance. Nia, just come with me to look at the portal. Do that for me at the very least, will you?"

Her heart pounding, Nia followed Pester out of the overhang. She was immediately struck by an intense, icy blast of wind—a wind which could only come from an imp lord bent on a dark purpose. Soon her hands and feet turned blue. She felt she was walking through a narrow tunnel with walls shutting in around her. As he flew, Pester pulled at her anxiously, leading her to a steep incline along an old rockslide. Nia didn't notice. She just followed.

All around, thunder from impish spells sent down loose rocks and dirt. The debris pelted her as she climbed. Agitated tears rolled down her dirty cheeks. Pester aided her by pointing out the best footholds, but the iciness quickly reached her core, and her whole body went numb. About halfway up, she collapsed on a boulder, overcome with sleepiness.

"Don't do that, Nia. Get up!" Pester cried. "You've got to keep moving!"

"It's s-so c-cold," Nia muttered, wrapping her arms around herself

"Come on! Back on your feet!" Pester whispered anxiously. He yanked at Nia's hand. "Look, I can't do this. I can't shield you from this cold right now, you understand? I'd overexert myself like my mother did."

Nia looked at Pester. She could see his mouth moving, but his voice sounded far away. Her eyes were heavy. They began to close. *Sleep feels so good*, she thought. *What does it matter if I never reach the portal? It's not like Tanni would be there to go through with me.*

With that, Nia sighed contentedly. Her eyes shut fully. Then, another voice—not her own or the imp's—broke through. *On your feet*, said the voice. *You're almost there.*

It was Ease. Warmth flooded Nia's body as though she'd been submerged in a hot bath. Her teeth stilled. Joyfully, she opened her eyes, expecting the sprite's comforting form. But all she saw was Pester.

"Ease. Where's Ease?" she demanded. "She was just here."

"Snap out of it, girl!" Pester hissed. "I need you to stay with me."

Getting to her feet, Nia felt impervious to the cold. Her hands and feet were warm, and Lord Accuse's icy wind washed over her like a warm breeze. Looking at Pester, she said calmly, "I've snapped out of it. I'm coming."

Looking her over in astonishment, at first Pester couldn't believe his eyes. After a pause however, he muttered something about trans-realm spells, before pulling her again toward the portal.

"Trans-realms spells?" Nia asked. "I don't understand."

"Neither do I. But if there's one thing I'm learning about sprites, it's that when fully charged, they are far more powerful than we imps realize. It's just a theory, but I think Ease created a direct connection between herself and you when she opened a channel of communication with you in Shades. Now, it appears she cast some sort of cold protection on you, likely through that same connection."

"All the way from the Sunlands?" gasped Nia.

"Yes, even from the Sunlands, since I'm positive she's not here."

Pondering this, Nia climbed cautiously, moving between fallen trees and rocks.

"Wow, that's unbelievable," she finally said, her gratitude swelling.

"Yes, it is. But please stop thinking about it right now," Pester warned, "or we'll be detected."

Quickly, Nia made her thoughts more neutral. With the crest of the hill just overhead, she heard Pester tell her to duck and crawl in order to keep hidden by a natural scarp left after the landslide. The ground here was rough and uneven. After a few feet, she bit back a cry from kneeling on a sharp stone. Rubbing her bleeding knee, she continued following her imp. Pester led her a good fifty feet before stopping.

At the peak of the rockslide, people were shouting. "Retake the portal!" one voice yelled. "Don't let him cut us off from it!" another called.

Peering over the crevice lip, Nia felt her breath catch. The voices belonged to a beautiful, raven-haired people with strong, tall bodies. Six women and four men fought with fierce pride, their dazzling light pushing back their enemies. With magic shields that resembled flame, they blocked impish spells while two sprites threw blasts of light from behind them against the imp lord and his cronies. Mere feet from them, the imp lord was battling alongside some of the largest imps in the Shadelands. At almost twice the size of Pester, Lord Accuse outsized his cronies by several inches. His form was ugly and menacing. With cold, black eyes his gaze bore down on the Starbeams. Nia sensed he was trying to trap the Lightkeepers in his realm. The thought cut through the warming spell and chilled her to the bone.

Pointing to the right, Pester showed Nia another portal standing alone beyond the edge of the rockslide. It appeared unguarded. "There's your chance, Nia," he whispered. "You see how the others are completely distracted? Get up on my signal and run. Run as fast as you can out of this realm and back where you belong." The imp's throat caught. He looked away and feigned distraction. "Don't look back, okay?"

Nia stared at the portal, overwhelmed that the moment had arrived. But now the moment was tainted. Escape meant leaving Tanni behind—And Pester. She needed more time to decide what to do. Tapping her imp on the shoulder, she lowered her voice and said, "Pester, have you checked it to make sure it isn't a trap?"

"I can swear to you on every curse it isn't a trap," the imp replied.

"How do you know?" Nia asked, biting her lip.

Rolling his eyes, Pester hissed, "Because I checked it over thoroughly. I think the Lightkeepers have drawn Lord Accuse away from it to safeguard it. They don't want him to see it."

"Why are you in such a hurry to be rid of me?" Nia demanded, her heart throbbing.

"Stop, Nia. I told you," Pester said evenly, "don't focus on your emotions right now. You could get us killed."

Nia closed her eyes and let out a long sigh. "Did I upset you?" she asked calmly. "Is that why you just want me to go?"

"Not now, child. Look," Pester whispered urgently, "the coast is clear. Get up and go!"

"Why?"

"I said, go!"

Shaking her head, Nia crawled backward from the crest of the hill. Pester hissed in frustration, but she ignored it. Instead, she clambered down the crumbly hill, determined to avoid being forced by her imp to return. She was almost halfway down, when Pester flew in front of her, his expression furious.

"What are you doing? Get back up there, now!"

"All you want is to be rid of me. Why does everyone want to be rid of me?" Nia felt her anger start to boil over. "Tanni's still out there. I can save him, don't you see?"

Pester's angry expression contorted with fear. Pulling at her roughly, he sped her descent down the hill. "Say nothing," he whispered. "Don't even think. We're about to be spotted." Diving behind a large boulder, he compelled Nia to follow. Once in place, he mouthed to her, "Don't move!"

Just then, a deep voice called out nearby, "Oy, sir, I found another portal!"

Terrified shouts echoed from the Lightkeepers as they realized one of their last escape routes was in jeopardy. Nia's mind numbed with shock. Peering over the boulder, Pester was breathing hard. "All right," he said quietly, "go!"

Nia ran. Sliding down the loose gravel, she nearly fell twice before reaching more sure footing at the bottom. Then, she tore through the forest, running until her lungs burned. At last, she slid to a halt, gasping for air. By her side was Pester. He'd kept up with her the whole time, his mouth tight with controlled fury.

"Happy now?" he snarled. "You're completely trapped. You had your chance to escape, and you blew it!"

"I couldn't leave. Not without Tanni. Besides," Nia paused to catch her breath, "there'll be other Lightkeepers in the future."

"You can't be serious. Nia! Couldn't you see that Lord Accuse was trying to deal the Lightkeepers a fatal blow? He was trying to destroy them once and for all! You're stuck here. End of story.

And now, thanks to you, I'm stuck here with you too. I'll become a sprite, Lord Accuse will hear about it, he'll come looking for me, and we'll both be killed. Congratulations, girl. You've officially ruined everything!"

"Ruined what, Pester?" Nia demanded, taking a step toward the imp. "Your chance to go on hurting and controlling helpless Starbeams for millennia to come? Ruined your chance to be some sort of pawn for the imp lord? All you ever wanted me for was to be your convenient food source and free labor. That's all anyone here ever is. You never cared about me, did you? You lied when you said I'd be to you as a favored child, didn't you? Now that I'm no longer useful to you, you don't want me anymore. You're Shades-bent on getting rid of me once and for all!"

"Stop!" Pester gasped, his hand in the air. "That's not true. Just calm down, okay? You're tearing my skull to pieces with your emotions."

"No!" Nia cried. "I won't stop! What am I to you exactly? Do you even know how to care or are you too much of a creature of darkness?"

Pester dropped to his knees. Holding his head with both hands, he whimpered, "I'm begging you, Nia. Settle down so we can talk about this rationally."

"Answer me! What am I? Who am I?" Nia demanded, tears stinging her eyes. "Do you love me as a father loves his favored child? Have you ever loved me at all?"

Squirming, Pester started singing his lullaby as a feeble shield against her. The spell proved too great for him however, and his voice became steadily weaker and weaker.

Determined to get through to him, Nia said fiercely, "I knew what love was. It was Mother's soft voice. It was Father's gentle hands. My parents loved me with kindness. They comforted me when I feared they'd disappear. Not once did they try to leave me, even when it was clear they no longer wanted me."

In a flash, dozens of happy memories burst into Nia's brain. Her father picked her up to see a stream gurgling beneath a bridge. Her mother sewed a cloth doll for her to play with. They embraced her and dried her tears after scraping her knee. Her father made a flower crown and placed it on top of her head. He whispered, "You're my little angel," before tucking her into bed. Nia's heart swelled with a bittersweet happiness.

A scream broke her reverie. Thrashing in the dirt, Pester cried out, "This is it, Mother! To dust!" He screamed again as a flash of light burst through his body. Then, he fell silent and became still.

Nia ran to him and knelt by his side. "Pester?" she asked. "Pester, are you okay?" Looking at his chest, she gave a startled cry. His chest didn't move. "No! You can't be dead. Pester, come back!"

The imp remained still. Choking back tears, Nia lifted Pester's limp body and cradled him like a doll, rocking him back and forth and sobbing in despair. *Pester was right*, she thought. *He was right not to want me. This is what I do—I hurt others.* With the imp limp in her arms, Nia was alone in the Shadelands—abandoned, friendless, helpless, and trapped.

CHAPTER 23

Nothing mattered anymore. All was hopeless. Nia felt the darkness come on, and she welcomed it. What was the point of feeling when all it led to was pain? Drawing inward, the world around her slowly disappeared. All became numb, quiet, and still.

A sharp pain on the top of her head brought her back to reality. In bewilderment, she saw a pinecone fall from her head and roll along the ground in front of her. Still holding Pester's body, she grabbed the cone with numb fingers. It felt dull and lifeless. Despite this, she knew something important was connected with it, but she didn't know what. Shrugging, she gently placed Pester on the ground, and tucked the pinecone into her backpack.

The imp looked peacefully asleep. His ugly features had melted away now that he could no longer scowl, leaving only beauty behind. Nia let fresh tears fall. *If only I hadn't killed you*, she thought. *You might have made a wonderful sprite.* "Don't worry, Pester," she whispered mournfully. "I'll find a safe spot to bury you."

After putting the pack back on, she gingerly picked up Pester and got to her feet. If she was reading the sunlight through the canopy properly, it was late afternoon in the Shadelands.

"To the portals where the imp lord is," she said, imitating

Pester's voice without irony or humor. "Then to death."

Drawing inward, Nia realized she was finally getting what she'd always wanted back in Shades. She was numb. And it was not what she'd expected. It was—dissatisfying. As she retraced the steps she took in her retreat from the battle, she barely noticed the burning cuts on her feet or the windy chill that carried with it a steadily increasing rain. The dripping trees remained sinister and brooding, but she didn't care. She was a wanderer again, just as she had been when she was five. *If Lord Accuse doesn't kill me*, she mused, *perhaps another imp will find me and do what Pester never could.*

As if in response to the thought, an imp approached from somewhere beneath the gloomy trees. Nia waited for the creature impassively, expecting for it to leap upon her at any moment and put an end to her last conscious, miserable moments. She was determined to give it as much access to her mind as possible. *I'm so tired of feeling*, she thought.

Finally, the imp came into view. To Nia's surprise, it was Pester's sister, Wither.

"You!" cried Wither. Then, seeing her brother's limp body in Nia's arms, she muttered to herself, "Got a bit carried away with her emotions, did she?"

Nia hung her head, as Wither came closer. The imp peered over Pester's lifeless body. With a light hiss, she backed off. Thinking for a long moment, she at last said softly, "Looks like you could use a bit of guidance. Mind if I land on your shoulder and direct you for a bit?"

Nia shrugged, "Sure. Just don't treat me like a drudge."

"Interesting request. Where were you headed?"

"The hill where the battle took place," Nia said, pointing weakly. "I was hoping the imp lord would spot me."

"Oh—well, that sounds cheerful. Let me guess," Wither said, "you were just going to hand Pester's limp body over to Lord Accuse. Am I right?"

"I was gonna bury him," Nia said, grief cutting through the numbness.

Wither snorted. "You know," she said, pursing her lips, "you've got bigger priorities than that right now. Stick him in your pack and bury him tomorrow. He won't start stinking yet. At least, not any more than he did in life."

The imp had a point. Nia unslung her pack. Moving the pinecone aside, she placed Pester inside with a wet, shivering hand. Her heart ached. "All right," she said through chattering teeth, "where to?"

"To the place Lord Accuse and the Lightkeepers used to be," said Wither.

Nia started to comply. But thinking over Wither's statement, she asked dismally, "Used to be?"

"Yep. The Lightkeepers aren't there anymore. I watched Lord Accuse drive them out. He tried cornering them, but they combined their magic with the two sprites, and the whole hill lit up like a bonfire." Wither flailed her arms in the air for effect. "I had to duck behind a tree trunk to keep from being blasted myself. I didn't see what happened next, but I'm pretty sure the Lightkeepers escaped, closing the portal behind them. I'm not positive, but I believe only Lord Accuse survived the blast. He must have hidden behind something, because there's no way in Shades he would have survived being in the epicenter of that wave otherwise, even if he is an Original. After his defeat, he went off to sulk."

Nia responded to the story with more shivering. Wither tilted her head at her and said, "You look dreadful. You smell too. The Starbeams left behind a camp when they fled the Shadelands. Seems they planned on staying on that hill for quite a while, but I can't imagine why. Go up to the top of the hill and check it out."

Finished with her command, the imp took Pester's place on Nia's shoulder.

Sluggishly, Nia followed Wither's instructions through the pouring rain. The hill slowly came back into view. No flashes of light or thundering spells crackled through the air now. All was deathly quiet. Through the cold wetness, Nia mindlessly followed Wither's instructions to a winding trail on the hillside that had a steady incline. Listlessly she climbed, willingly manipulated by Wither's coaching. At the top, everything was blackened and charred from the battle. The trees appeared struck by lightning. They were missing several lower branches on the eastward facing side. Just as Wither had said, there was no sign of any portals. Nearby, the remains of an abandoned camp—complete with tents, a firepit, and chairs—appeared untouched by the fight. The small encampment looked as if the former occupants would return at any moment.

"Finally," Wither said. "Took you long enough. See? The Lightkeepers are gone and so is Lord Accuse."

"I'm glad the Lightkeepers made it," Nia muttered half-heartedly. "Hopefully they don't try to come back. I wouldn't want to see what other things Lord Accuse wants to throw at them."

"He wants to throw a fair number of things at them, for sure. Whether they come back for it or not is on them," Wither chuckled darkly. "Hey, see the chairs by the firepit? Sit in one of them. I need you rested so you can keep carrying me."

Detached from the scene before her, Nia walked through the drizzle to the chairs, unslung her pack, took Pester out, and propped him up in an empty seat.

"What are you doing?"

"Bringing a sense of normalcy," said Nia, as she eased into the chair next to her dead imp. While she sat, her mind slowly went blank. Wither remained quiet.

All at once, Nia burst out of the blankness. Every emotion she was trying to avoid by going numb flooded through her, the most poignant being self-rage and despair. Doubling over, she began to sob. Vaguely, she saw Wither fall from her shoulder into the firepit. "What a terrible mess I've made!" Nia wept. "Pester, you warned me, but I didn't listen. You screamed, but I ignored it. My own selfishness killed you. I'm so, so sorry! Everyone I touch ends up hurting or dead. How could I be so worthless?"

"Please, Nia—stop!" Moaned Wither. Coated in ash, the imp held her temples and stumbled among the remains of the campfire. "You're tearing me to pieces."

Nia choked back her grief with deep, soothing breaths.

Fluttering from the firepit to the chair beside Nia, Wither wiped the damp ash from her arms and sighed, "You need some kind of cleansing activity. Look at you, you're filthy! Just like Pester never to make you bathe. Like imp, like drudge. I think you should rid yourself of the filth of Shades once and for all."

Becoming aware of the dark water streaming out of her hair, and seeing her arms caked with wet, muddy coal dust, Nia nodded. Never had she felt so disgusted to be in her own skin.

"Wait a moment," said Wither, holding up a hand. "Before I send you to bathe, let me zap whatever bugs are on you first. If I'm gonna keep your shoulder warm, I'd rather not continue to share space with lice and fleas. Hold still."

The imp grimaced as she grabbed Nia's filthy arm. A sudden staticky feeling made Nia jump. A moment later she squealed as dozens of small bugs dropped from her hair. Wither brushed her hands together in satisfaction. Then, pointing to Nia's right, she grinned, "There's a pool over there. Go give yourself a bath. Scrub the grime away. You'll smell better."

Without hesitation, Nia dashed to the pool. Staring at its shallow depths for a few seconds, her heart pounding, she jumped in and gasped at the shocking cold that enveloped her. Gritting her teeth, she attacked her skin with sand from the shore, scrubbing off years of dirt and coal. As she squeezed and pulled at her matted black hair, the pool clouded over and became nearly black with grime and dead bugs. Still, she scrubbed—attacking the stains on her hands and arms, face, feet, and legs until they smarted. Her teeth were chattering, and her body was nearly frozen through, but she didn't notice until she climbed out of the water.

Standing in the rain, Nia considered her ragged clothes. Hot fury flooded through her as she remembered taking them off a corpse. Agonized, she tore them off in disgust.

Stripped of everything remaining from her life in Shades, Nia wanted nothing more than a place to hide. But she couldn't even get privacy. At that moment, Wither landed on her shoulder and patted her cheek. "You do smell better. Excellent," the imp said condescendingly. "Go to the tent nearest the trail. It belonged to one of the women who was in the encampment."

Shivering violently, Nia complied. She walked through the mud to the tent Wither had indicated. Inside, she found it clean and dry, with a bedroll and soft sheets. Beside the head of the bed was a lady's hairbrush and comb. On the other side was a small trunk. Wither pointed out a towel hanging near the entrance. Nia grabbed it and toweled off while the imp rested on the bedroll.

Frowning at the amount of dirt she'd missed, she watched Wither open the trunk and beckon her over. Wrapping the towel around herself, she came and knelt down beside the imp. Inside the trunk were neatly folded piles of long-sleeved, woolen lady's tunics, clean linen undergarments, a belt, and woolen pants. Nia smiled. The clothes reminded her of her last happy moments with Tanni.

"Try on the green one," suggested Wither. "It's my favorite color."

She has a favorite color? Nia wondered, grabbing the emerald tunic and holding it out in front of her. Whoever owned this before had been very tall. Nia would have to wear it as a dress. Setting it aside, she tested out the undergarments, which for a grown woman would have been shorts almost reaching the knee.

On her, they were a bit loose, hanging just below mid-calf. But if she cinched them up with the belt, she could get along fine. When she pulled on the tunic-dress, it was baggy and cumbersome. The sleeves hung loose, but she was determined to wear it. After all, it at least didn't come off a dead body. Rolling the sleeves up to her wrists, she was satisfied. The fresh clothes had another effect— She'd stopped shivering.

"That doesn't look entirely terrible. It's certainly better than those rags Pester had you wearing before. Speaking of," Wither chuckled, looking out of the tent, "get my brother out of the rain. I know he needed a shower too, but he doesn't need to be buried at sea."

Nia went immediately, her heart heavy. She picked up Pester's frozen body and carried him into the tent. Laying him on the bedroll, she then covered him with the sheets as if he were just sleeping.

"Very nice," Wither muttered sarcastically.

Grabbing the comb and brush next to her brother, Wither told Nia to pilfer the other tents. Nia started to comply. But noticing Tanni's soaked pack on a chair, she carried it to the awning of Pester's tent and left it there so it could dry out. Satisfied, she went back to exploring.

The other tents had much the same contents as the first, the only difference being that four contained men's things. Having saved the smallest for last, Nia peered inside and felt her breath catch. It was a storeroom. Inside were hanging ham hocks, wheels of cheese, boxes of fruits and vegetables, wine casks, loads and loads of hard biscuits, and a jelly that looked to contain meat.

Stepping inside this wonder shelter, Nia simply stared. "I don't deserve this," she muttered. "I don't deserve any of it."

"Nonsense," Wither cackled. "You're all skin and bones. Eat, Nia. How are you supposed to carry me otherwise?"

Frowning, Nia obeyed. It was nearly dark when she made her

way barefoot through the rain and mud to Tanni's pack. Taking it into a lady's tent next to Pester's, she sat down on the bedroll, feeling utterly exhausted. She thought of lying down, but something told her she should open the pack first. There, sitting on top of sodden loaves and soaked meat, gray and worn out, was the pinecone. Nia ran a finger over its frayed surface, trying to remember how it got into her pack in the first place. Then, it came to her.

"Ugh," she muttered. "Pinecones—everywhere I go. What does it even mean?" She gnawed on the inside of her cheek. "It fell on my head. I could have sworn there was some kind of meaning behind it. Now, I can't figure out why. If Pester were alive, he'd tell me to get rid of it. Perhaps, maybe, I should."

"I'd say the same," replied a voice.

Nia started. She'd forgotten Wither was sitting on her shoulder.

"That thing's worthless," the imp said. "You don't need a silly, old pinecone anyway."

Nia went to the tent entrance and pulled back her arm, preparing to throw the cone. But her arm stopped abruptly as if something held it back. There was indeed meaning here. It just wasn't obvious. Something told her she'd figure it out if she was just patient.

"I don't know why, but I can't get rid of it quite yet. I'll tell you why when I figure it out," said Nia.

"Whatever," Wither snorted.

Nia rolled her eyes. Tossing the cone at the foot of the bed, she sat down. Wither then hopped off her shoulder and instructed her to take the comb and brush. "Your hair needs help," she explained. Nia attacked her matted hair. She managed to free some tangles, but others couldn't be helped. Wither told her she'd have to cut them out.

Worn out from this activity, Nia laid down on the surprisingly soft bed. The last thing she saw before drifting off was the pinecone fading into the shadows of the night.

CHAPTER 24

Just after dawn, Nia awoke, warm and comfortable for the first time since she could remember. In the dim light, she sat up in the tent, reflecting on the previous day. Wither had led her here. The imp had bathed, clothed, fed, and housed her. She had rid her of the bugs on her body. In all ways she had been remarkably helpful so far. Nia was grateful, but she couldn't quite understand it. Yes, Pester's sister was part sprite, but not enough for her motives to be entirely pure. With Pester gone, why hadn't Wither taken full control of her and left her mind in utter ruin? The creature didn't seem honorable enough to heed Nia's request that she not be treated as a drudge.

Pondering this for a moment, it came to her. *No, she's not being honorable*, Nia mused. *Wither is acting on different motives. She's preparing me for my next move. The imp is anxious to have her revenge.*

Feeling someone watching her, Nia looked to her right and jumped. Wither sat there, her black eyes almost brooding. "Have you been there this whole time?" asked Nia, clutching her chest.

"Yep. I'm surprised you didn't notice me before," said Wither, chuckling. Then, her expression grew serious. "You had some sort of a breakthrough. Tell me about it."

Nia blushed. Clearing her throat, she said shyly, "Your motives. I think I figured out your motives."

"Oh?" Wither said eagerly. "Do tell!"

"You've been helping me and being nice to me because you're trying to get me built up enough to have a showdown with Vex," said Nia, her heart hammering at the thought. "Am I right?"

Wither clapped her hands in delight and crowed, "Ooh, I love how intelligent you are! Yes, those are my primary motives, I'll admit. But I must say, there was at least one more. See if you can figure it out."

"Well . . ." Nia looked at the imp's healthy features. "You're also using me as a food source, aren't you?"

Wither giggled and nodded. Patting Nia's shoulder, she cried, "And I didn't even have to work for it! You were so depressed, I just had to keep you moving. And you know what? It worked."

Nia scowled. Like Pester, everything Wither did was with double motives. Getting to her feet in frustration, she stretched and prepared to leave. When Wither asked what she was doing, she snapped, "Going to go hang out with Pester for a while. Being dead, he's through with using me, unlike some people."

"Hey!" Wither hollered. "If you recall, you gave me your express permission to guide you yesterday. I was only doing what you asked me to."

The imp landed heavily on Nia's shoulder. Despite her agitation, Nia didn't shake her off. She had a point after all. Outside the tent, the rain had stopped. With much of the canopy on the hill blasted away by the battle, hints of blue sky peeked through. The sight startled her. Staring up at the morning sunlight glinting off the tops of the trees, her wonder increasing, she heard Wither hiss suddenly. Then, the imp darted off her shoulder. Confused, Nia turned to see a small, bright form exiting Pester's tent.

Nia's heart skipped. Tears started in her eyes. "Ease?" she cried joyfully. "Ease, Is that you?"

"What?" asked a familiar voice. It wasn't Ease.

"Pester?" Nia's jaw dropped.

Pester's fiery eyes looked Nia up and down. "Nia?" he asked, sounding uncertain.

Nia nodded and walked toward him to take in his bright face. She was overwhelmed by the transformation of his features. No ugliness remained. He was Pester still, but a softened version, as if the care lines were rubbed off his formerly gray skin. There was no sense of skin color now. He was simply light. His wings, which previously resembled those of bats, appeared be made of thin, clear crystal. Most startling were his eyes. They weren't dark, black pits anymore. They were hot coals with no hint of malice within their depths.

Presently, Pester realized Nia was staring at him. Curious why, he looked himself over and gasped. Rubbing the back of his glowing head, he peered at Nia and asked, "Are we dead or alive?"

"Alive," said Nia confidently. Joy filled her heart. Then, something landed on her shoulder.

"Can you tone your emotions down, Nia?" Wither grumbled. "I'd like to keep my impish form for a bit longer if you don't mind. Pester, you look awful."

"You're too kind," said Pester gruffly. "Normally I'd tell you the same, but right now I feel—well, I don't feel quite myself."

Wither huffed. A light wind ruffled a nearby tent. At length, Nia broke the silence. "I'm so sorry, Pester. I didn't mean to cause this. I thought—I thought I'd killed you."

"I thought you did too," Pester said. "Frankly, I'm surprised you didn't. Last thing I remember was my head feeling like it was gonna explode. How long ago was that?"

"Yesterday," said Nia, her cheeks burning. "It all happened yesterday."

"Yesterday?" Pester crossed his arms. "You know, if I were still an imp, I'd probably be furious with you right now. But weirdly enough, I don't feel that mad. That doesn't mean I don't have a bone to pick with you, though. Why didn't you listen to me yesterday and leave the Shadelands like you were supposed to? And why is Wither sitting on your shoulder as if she owns you?"

Nia opened her mouth to speak, but Wither cut her off, laughing, "Finders, keepers, brother!"

Pester shook his head. Flying toward Nia, he kept his fiery gaze steadily on his sister. As he approached, Wither cowered into Nia's hair. *What is Pester planning to do?* Nia wondered. *Is he going to burst into light and fry his sister?*

Now level with Wither, Pester said in a quiet, authoritative voice, "Off. Now."

With a barely audible squeak, Wither hopped into the air. Once she got her distance, she turned back with a snarl and hissed, "I was just keeping her shoulder warm for you. A lot cleaner shoulder now, might I add? Geez, Pester, don't get your wings in a tangle!"

Pester continued staring down his sister. Nia watched the standoff uneasily. At last, she said timidly, "Wither has been a great help to me, Pester. Please don't chase her off." Then, looking from him to his sister, she pleaded, "And please, Wither, don't tell Lord Accuse about us. I still have to rescue Tanni, remember?"

"I wasn't planning on it," Wither snorted. "Though I might relish it if Pester doesn't stop acting more 'cursed than thou.'"

"Fine," Pester sighed. "Wither, don't go yet. Stick around for a bit, alright?"

Though scowling, Wither nodded. Pester turned to eye Nia. Pressing against her ear, he whispered softly. "I have a few things I'd like to talk to you about." Leaning back, he spoke in full volume. "Wither, mind giving us some space for a minute?"

Nia's heart sank. She didn't relish the conversation Pester wanted to have with her. Wither didn't seem excited about it either. The imp huffed and flew to a nearby chair. "Talk away. Don't mind me," she said through gritted teeth.

"Come with me to where the battle took place," Pester said. He craned his neck in the desired direction. "We can talk there."

The ground was black and charred. Ashen pine needles crunched underfoot. Remaining branches on the forlorn trees swayed slightly in a cool breeze. Pester flew beside Nia, his expression grim. Reaching the spot where the hidden portal had been, he pointed to a lone boulder near the area of the rockslide and told Nia to sit down. When he landed next to her, Nia turned away to view the crumbled hillside.

"Look at me, Nia."

Nia squeezed her eyes shut. Eventually, she pivoted until, sitting cross-legged, she met Pester's fiery gaze.

Pester rubbed the back of his head and sighed, "We're in kind of a quandary. You ran yesterday. Now these portals are closed forever. I tried to save you, but you wouldn't let me. You tried to kill me, but I wouldn't let you. Let's just say I haven't raised you very well."

Nia pursed her lips as she relived the pain of Pester's near fatal argument with her. "You know why I didn't leave," she said, pausing to hold back tears. "Tanni needed saving. So did you."

"So did I?" cried Pester.

"Yes! Just imagine if you had given in and joined the imp lord when he asked you to. You'd be dead right now, just like the twenty-odd imps that battled with him on this hill. Following the combined blast of the Starbeams and sprites, you'd be nothing but dust blowing in the wind," Nia said, crossing her arms and glaring at him.

"How do you know that? How do you even know how the battle ended?" asked Pester incredulously.

"Because Wither witnessed it," Nia explained. "She hid behind a tree when the blast came. I have a feeling Lord Accuse escaped by hiding behind this very rock. The Lightkeepers and sprites escaped and closed the portals behind them. As I was saying, though, if you had been among Lord Accuse's cronies, you really would be dead."

Pester was silent for a long moment. Then, he exhaled heavily and said thoughtfully, "If the Lightkeepers escaped, there's still hope for you."

"And for Tanni, and for you."

"For me?" cried Pester. "How in Shades is there hope for me?"

"You're a sprite now," Nia said firmly. "If I go through the portal, you do too."

Pester's eyes widened. He slowly sat down.

"I may never know whether you ever loved me. But know this," Nia said, a tear streaking down her cheek. "A favored daughter doesn't abandon her father. You can curse me till your light goes out, but I won't abandon you, not even should I face all the world or Lord Accuse himself."

Utterly floored, Pester rubbed one ear feverishly and choked, "I don't deserve this, Nia. I don't deserve any of it. Certainly not your compassion, kindness, or friendship. I was terrible to you. You want to know just how terrible?" At this, Pester clasped his hands toward Nia, as if in supplication. "My thoughts yesterday were, 'How could I have ever loved someone I never saw as my equal in the first place?' You were my food source and status symbol. That was it. I treated you as a favored child mechanically, not emotionally. I fulfilled the letter of the law, but not the matter of the heart. How can you say you won't abandon me when I am this? When this is all I have ever been, and ever will be?"

Watching Pester shake with pent up emotion, Nia felt raw. Drawing in a deep breath, she said softly, "That's what the Shadelands made you to be. Come back into the light, Pester. It's who you really are."

Burying his face in his hands, Pester shuddered violently. Composing himself, he whispered, "I'm sorry. I'm so sorry."

As he spoke, Pester's light increased, and Nia's skin began

glowing. Warmth crept through her, as if an undiscovered void had filled up. Overcome with amazement, her joy was rudely interrupted when her pinecone, tossed by a disgruntled Wither, hit her square in the head. "Ow!" Nia rubbed her scalp as the cone rolled onto the ground. To her surprise, the cone was open, revealing rows and rows of seeds.

The effect of hitting her with the cone wasn't quite what Wither had anticipated. Instead, Nia stared at it, feeling once again that it must be important. Slowly, the meaning of it dawned on her and the glow of her skin grew even brighter. Wither hissed in annoyance and retreated back to her chair to sulk.

Picking up the cone, Nia put a hand on Pester's tiny, glowing shoulder. He glanced at her light and startled.

"I forgive you completely," Nia said. "Like a pinecone that drops dead from a tree, the old you has died. But every cone contains seeds. Those seeds have sprouted into new life. Welcome to that life, Pester."

The two of them sat in silence for a while. Nia stared at the blue sky and the dark, endless forest beneath the hill. Somewhere out there, Tanni would soon be fought over. When that happened, she was determined to rescue him.

CHAPTER 25

It was three hours after dawn when Nia and Pester at last returned to Wither, who still sulked in her chair in front of the cold firepit. She greeted the pair sourly and folded her arms in disgust. "You two look worse than ever," she insisted, eyes glittering with jealousy. "You're so ugly now it almost hurts to look at you."

"It's not too late, sister," Pester said with a knowing smirk. "You could be glowing too, you know."

"I'd rather rot," Wither scowled. "Besides, you two need to get out of here. You're already late."

Nia grabbed a chair and set it up across from Wither. Sitting down and catching Wither's dark eye, she took a couple deep breaths before saying nervously, "Wither, I'd like you to come with us to help find Tanni."

Wither eyed her suspiciously. "Why would I want to do that?"

"Because it's your revenge—not mine. Besides, Pester isn't quite sure where the Battle Marsh is. He's stumped why you would think he does."

"Are you kidding me?" Wither spun toward Pester. "You don't know where the marsh is? Are you dense?"

Pester landed on a chair next to his sister and met her

exasperated gaze with an abnormally patient expression. Wither searched his face with annoyance and hissed at him. Pester smiled. Finally, he replied dryly, "You know, you're right, Wither. I am dense. I'm nowhere near as cunning as you. Your greatness far exceeds mine. I'm brainless to not know where the Battle Marsh is. I need help—lots of it. I've lived my life with my head stuck under a boulder."

"More like smashed by one," Wither sighed crossly. But her mouth turned up at the corners. Staring at the ground, she huffed loudly, "Fine. I'll lead Nia to the marsh. But you owe me for this, Pester."

"What could I possibly give to you now? It's not like I can set you up with a new drudge. Besides, one look at me by Lord Accuse and I'd be dead!"

Wither laughed hollowly, "All too true. Share some of your energy with me, then. I feel empty."

Pester's brow furrowed. "But you're not a sprite!" he exclaimed. "The energy would bounce right out of you and possibly knock you silly."

"Maybe. But I almost want to make it work. It's not fair," Wither whined. "Why do you get to be more powerful than me?"

Nia's heart lifted. Wither would lead them to the marsh. She hadn't bothered the imp by asking. Getting to her feet, she thanked Wither and went to pack food for the trek.

Inside her tent, Nia grabbed Tanni's pack, then brought it outside to a sudden drop in the hill a few paces from camp. Emptying the moist, spoiled food over the drop, she watched in satisfaction as it tumbled down the hill. Returning to the tent, she grabbed the towel and dabbed the pack dry. Then, she packed her comb and hairbrush at the bottom. Moving on to the storage tent, she filled the remaining space with stores of food. She was just fitting a small wheel of cheese into the top portion of the pack, when the storeroom illuminated, and she saw a flash of light brighten the camp through the open flap of the tent.

Around the firepit, Pester gasped and Wither screeched. Wondering what all the commotion was about, Nia dashed out of the tent and turned to look in the direction of the light. Approximately fifty yards away, a tiny portal stood open, the dazzlingly bright head of a man peering through. Just behind him was a green field dotted with wildflowers. Backing from the portal, he allowed a small, bright form to enter the Shadelands. As soon as the shining form came through, the strange man waved his hand and the portal collapsed, hiding him from view. Staring at the dazzling creature, Nia was rooted to the spot, unsure what to do. Suddenly, the creature locked eyes with her and flew her way.

Unable to do anything else, Nia fell to her knees and lowered her gaze before the fast-approaching light. She'd just begun to glow herself, but her own light felt dull and inadequate before such brilliance. In the space of three shaky breaths, the creature landed in front of her. The tiny figure cleared her throat and then—

"Nia," she said, "it's me."

Nia's heart leapt. "Ease?" she cried. "But you're so bright! How could it be you?"

Ease laughed softly, "Being home does that to a person." Then, her expression darkened. "But Nia, why didn't you come home too? Why did you ignore the open portal? I could sense you heading right for it, and I alerted the Lightkeepers. They kept the extra portal hidden and secret just for you. They fought the battle with Lord Accuse on this very hill for the sole purpose of saving you. You were mere feet from it. Why did you turn and run?"

Kneeling speechless before the sprite, Nia momentarily forgot about Pester and Tanni. Her hesitation to leave the Shadelands seemed pointless now, especially considering the trouble she'd caused the Lightkeepers who were trying to rescue her. Lowering her head in shame, she started to apologize, when Pester landed on her shoulder. Ease's breath caught in surprise.

"P—Pester?" she stammered. "You're a sprite?"

"Surprised?" Pester smiled. "Yes, I'm a sprite now. And to answer your question, I'm part of the reason Nia hesitated. I am what I have become because of her hesitation."

Looking at Nia, Ease asked, "Is this true?"

Nia nodded, "I hesitated for two reasons, really. For Pester, yes, but also for Tanni." Placing a hand over her heart, she said firmly, "I won't leave the Shadelands without him."

"Then I'm afraid coming home won't be an option for you," Ease said sadly. "Tanni is trapped in a mine, Nia. How you expect to save him from there is beyond me. Surely Pester can tell you that."

"He's not in a mine," Wither yelled, peeking out from behind the storage tent. "He's headed to a marsh."

"And who are you—an imp of this realm?" Ease shook her head in disbelief. "What do Tanni's whereabouts matter to you, and how can I be certain you're telling me the truth?"

At this, Wither zoomed out from behind the tent, her hands balled into fists. Landing next to Nia, she crossed her arms, looked Ease up and down, and growled, "Try me."

Ease studied her calmly. Then, her eyebrows shot up and she said, "It appears I was mistaken. You really do know where Tanni is. From the look of you, you're Pester's kin. Am I right?"

"Not by choice," Wither said, rolling her eyes.

"She's my sister," Pester explained.

Feeling her knees start to ache, Nia got to her feet and timidly asked everyone to join her at the chairs where they could continue their conversation. To her relief, all complied without complaint. Once at the firepit, she sank gratefully into a chair, and the sprites and imp settled on others in a circle across from her. Being small, they remained standing on their seats.

Gathering her thoughts, Nia turned to Ease and said shyly, "Wither says Tanni's been stolen from Vex and is being taken to a place called the Battle Marsh to be fought over." Nia turned from Ease to the only imp in the group. "Am I right, Wither?"

"I don't lie," said Wither, glaring at Ease. Then, thinking about her statement for a moment, she amended, "At least not when revenge is on the line."

Ease shifted from one leg to the other. "Revenge?" she wondered. "Why do you want revenge?"

Seeing that Wither was losing patience, Nia took over. She explained about Vex killing Wither's drudge following his exile from Shades. Then, she told how Wither volunteered to guide them to the marsh so she could steal Tanni and leave Vex empty-handed. Ease made a good audience, only interrupting for clarification.

When Nia had finished, Ease turned to Wither and asked, "When do we need to get going?"

"A half hour ago," Wither said irritably.

"Are we too late then?"

"Not if we hurry," Wither growled.

Nia's heart raced. Turning to Wither, she asked, "How far away is it, and when do you expect Tanni to be brought there?"

Wither considered the question. "It's a little less than a day-and-a-half journey as the imp flies—that is, if the imp takes a break. But you're a clumsy, bumbling Starbeam. If you'd left when I first told you to, you'd have made it just fine. But you just had to dilly dally, didn't you? Good luck getting your friend now."

"I told you I don't know where the marsh is!" Pester cried. "If she had left when you told her to, we'd probably be lost!"

From her chair, Ease held up a hand. Nia met her eyes. The memory of running with Tanni flashed through Nia's mind, and she thought she understood what the sprite was planning. "We still have a chance to get there on time," Ease said. "If I cast wingfoot on Nia, we'd probably get there by nightfall tonight."

"Yeah," Wither said testily, "but what about the rest of us? We can't all fit on her shoulder."

"If I could still cast jetflight, that wouldn't be a problem," sighed Pester. "But my magic isn't working right now. I don't know how to cast anything anymore."

"Don't you?" asked Ease in surprise. "Focus on the spell but use light to illuminate it. See if you can make it work that way."

Wither crossed her arms and stared at Pester. "This," she muttered, "I got to see."

"Wither, I suggest you hide behind a tent for just a moment," Ease warned. "Pester doesn't know his own strength yet. None of us do."

Wither scoffed. But thinking the better of it, she ducked behind a tent. Nia chuckled when she noticed the imp peeking out from behind it in curiosity.

Closing his eyes, Pester cautiously raised a hand to his chest, his face twisting in concentration. Nia and Ease tensed in anticipation. Wither held a hand over her face. But nothing happened.

"Can I come back?" Wither called. "Looks like brother can't—"

A brief, brilliant flash of light illuminated the camp, with Pester at its center. Wither squeaked. For a brief moment Nia thought fearfully that the imp had been fried. However, a moment later, she saw Wither alight on her chair. *Thank the stars*, Nia thought in relief.

"Did it work?" Wither wondered, her voice shaky.

Slowly, Pester opened his eyes. Then, shooting out of his chair, he zoomed at breathtaking speed around the perimeter of the camp, whooping in delight. Following a few laps, he landed back on his chair with a flourish, his face exuberant and satisfied.

"Congratulations," said Ease, smiling. "Since it's an impish spell, do you think Wither can cast it too?"

"No," said Pester, alarmed.

"And why not?" Wither demanded.

"Because you've broken your word a few too many times, Sister," said Pester. His eyes locked with hers in warning.

Wither clenched her teeth and sank angrily into her chair.

"Don't you mind that, Wither. Nia has two shoulders. She can carry us both," Ease said, eyeing Nia. "If she's willing, that is."

"More like, if I'm willing to share drudge space with a sprite," Wither grumbled.

"If you want your revenge, you'll have to," said Ease.

"Fine. Let's get going already," Wither snarled, waving a hand. "Get your pack, Nia. Let's go."

"Gladly," Nia smiled. She felt a change in the energy around her as she grabbed Tanni's pack from the storage tent. *This is really happening!*

When Nia rejoined them, Ease landed on her shoulder and cast the running spell on her. Immediately, energy pulsed through her body. Hopping from one foot to the other, she prepared to shoot off.

Ease called to Wither, suggesting she take Nia's empty shoulder. The imp let out a few curses but finally complied. It felt weird to Nia to have two such different energies on her shoulders, one light and one dark. The dissonance it created in her mind was almost overwhelming. Gathering her thoughts, she asked Wither where to go.

Without fanfare, Wither simply pointed. Nia took off with Pester keeping pace alongside her. Wind whistled in her ears. The landscape blurred around her. At the bottom of the hill, she turned southwest. Finally, she was going to get Tanni—albeit out from under the nose of a potentially dangerous opponent. *But perhaps,* she thought hopefully, *our rescue won't end up drawing Vex's attention.*

CHAPTER 26

Only twice did the group stop on their trek to the Battle Marsh. Once so Nia could gather water and eat, and once to renew wingfoot and jetflight. Whether going or stopping, Wither complained the entire time—especially when the rain began at midday. Ease showed remarkable patience with the imp. Nia's own patience was wearing thin, kept in check only by her desire to avoid unwanted attention.

The Wanderer's Forest seemed to last an eternity. Occasionally a small clearing popped up, but it zipped past before Nia realized she'd run through it. By late afternoon, she was soaked through from the rain and overwhelmed with claustrophobia. The trees were suffocating. At times, they seemed almost alive with darkness, bent on closing in around their prey and entrapping them. They grew especially ominous with two sprites and a Starbeam passing just beneath their canopy. Of the travelers, only Wither appeared unbothered by them. The trees were the one thing she didn't complain about.

Around twilight, the trees finally thinned out. Nia relaxed. She even started to cheer up a bit, until she was struck with a putrid, sulphureous smell. The songs of countless frogs echoed nearby.

Choking on the stench, she slowed and covered her nose with her damp sleeve. "What is that?"

"Battle Marsh," Wither said, perking up. "We're on the eastern end. We need to skirt it westward a bit. I'll tell you when you've reached the right spot."

"How do you know about this place, Wither?" asked Pester.

"Not all my drudges were taken honorably," Wither said lightly.

"You mean you stole one, fought over it, and lived to tell about it?" exclaimed Pester. "When was this?"

"About fifteen years ago," Wither replied casually. "My second mine drudge was dead, so I needed another one."

"Wait, I think this rings a bell. So, that's the real reason why you disappeared from the southern mines for a couple of weeks?" said Pester, eyeing his sister. "I had no idea."

Nia heard the imp chuckle. She hadn't realized Wither was a thief. "How did the battle end?" she asked cautiously. "Did your opponent give up?"

"No. They didn't get the chance to," Wither said darkly. Nia's blood ran cold. Wither was also a killer.

Pester grimaced at his sister. "You scare me sometimes."

"That's the whole point," Wither snickered.

Ease grasped Nia's hair, her breath increasing in tempo. Innocently, Nia asked, "Do all battles over drudges end this way?"

"No, some losers get a free kitten," cried Wither sarcastically. "Yes, girl. That's the law of this land. No apologies."

No one replied. In silence, Nia jogged through the darkening twilight, her hair dripping from the drizzling rain.

A little over an hour after dusk, Wither announced they'd reached the site to which Tanni would be brought. The chorus of frogs was almost deafening. Nia looked out at the noisome bog shrouded in darkness and shivered. In the circle of light cast by her and the two sprites, small skeletons littered the sodden ground. In a nearby pool, a dead imp floated face down. Nia turned from the sight. She felt she was going to be sick.

"Merciful stars, what place is this?" asked Ease from Nia's right shoulder. On the opposite shoulder, Wither giggled.

"Has anyone realized we're out in the open like sitting frogs?" Pester asked over the amphibian din. "Are we going to wait here until someone spots us?"

"Good call," Wither said loudly. "Follow me." With that, she hopped off Nia's shoulder and flew away from the marsh, back toward the trees. "There's a cave where we can hide out. It's the driest corner I know of around here. I brought my drudge there after I won."

With Wither's spot now vacant on Nia's shoulder, Pester landed there. As Nia jogged, Ease asked in a low voice, "Can we trust your sister—that she isn't leading us into a trap?"

"She knows the deep magic of this realm as well as anyone," Pester said grimly. "Magically speaking, if she betrays us, she'll doubly regret it. Betraying a family member is one part. Betraying those you've agreed to provide services for is another."

"Ease," Nia whispered, "Wither is a thief and a murderer. Is there any hope for her?"

"There's always hope," Ease said quickly, "but she has to learn regret first."

It was growing late when the group reached the cave's narrow entrance. Nia squeezed through. Inside was a low ceiling and just enough space for her to stretch out in. But it was dry, which was all that mattered. Ease and Pester stood on either side of her. Wither remained as sentinel at the entrance.

"There aren't any bears that might chase us out of here, are there?" asked Ease, glancing around the dimly lit cave.

"No," replied Wither and Pester in unison. Wither scowled, so Pester allowed her to explain. Sticking her tongue out at him, she turned to Ease and said in a mock teacher tone, "Drudges, are the only wildlife the Shadelands have left."

No bears was something of a comfort. Ignoring Wither's slight, Nia asked, "Why is that?"

"Because in the first five hundred years before the portals reopened, the imps used up the other wildlife as an energy source. When they went extinct," Wither said, giving Nia a knowing look, "the imps turned to a better food source."

Shuddering, Nia turned her thoughts elsewhere. "If Vex sees me grab Tanni tomorrow, what should I do?" she wondered.

The question bounced ominously off the cave walls. It was answered by Wither scoffing, "Run."

"No need to worry," Pester insisted. "Vex is under me now. I'll keep him in line."

Wither rolled her eyes but said nothing. Eventually, it was decided that if Wither and Pester sensed the imps and Tanni coming, Nia would be awakened immediately. In the meantime, the girl needed sleep. Ease cast a quick drying spell to keep Nia from getting chilled. Not long after that, she fell asleep to the droning voices of her companions.

When Nia opened her eyes, she felt as if mere minutes had passed. Two sprites and an imp were shaking her, whispering urgently for her to get up. Sitting up stiffly, she squinted at the dim light pouring in through the entrance of the cave.

"Have they reached the marsh?" she asked, stretching and yawning.

"They're close," said Pester. Nia reached for her pack. "No," Pester said urgently, "leave that here. It'll just slow you down. Ease, do you have a concealment spell you can use on her?" In the dim light, his expression looked almost anxious. Next to him, Wither's eyes glittered with a dark purpose.

"Yes, I have one," Ease said. "But Wither, for your own good, I'd advise you to stand back. Following your disclosure last night about your more shady past, I'm worried about any light accidentally blasting through you."

"Whatever," Wither sighed angrily, flying toward the cave entrance.

"Nia, I'm not sending you out there unguarded," Ease said, grabbing her arm. The sprite's voice was warm and comforting, calming Nia's pounding heart. "Pester and I are coming with you. Wither can make her choice about what she wants to do from here."

Nia looked down and gasped. She turned her hands over once, twice, three times. But they weren't there.

"Oh, I'm coming. I'm not gonna miss this," cried Wither, blinking out of sight.

Then, just like her hands and Wither, Ease and Pester vanished too. The hair on Nia's neck stood on end. "How will I know you're still with me?" she asked nervously.

"We're with you," Ease promised. "Let's go."

Nia lumbered out of the cave, a task made more difficult by not knowing where her limbs were in relation to the space around her. Once in the early daylight, Wither hissed in her ear, "Hurry up. They're almost at the edge of the marsh."

Ease and Pester landed on Nia's shoulders. Her heart leapt into her throat. A mere hundred yards off, Tanni stumbled toward the Battle Marsh, his once-new tunic blackened with coal and mud, his shoulders bent. In front of him flew Vex and another imp of the same size. Burning with indignation, Nia felt strength arise in her shaking limbs. *I will rescue Tanni or die*, she thought. *There's no other way around it.*

"They're getting ready to fight now. If we hurry," Pester whispered into Nia's ear, "we'll make it."

Nia picked up the pace, quickly learning how to move her unseen body. That is, until Ease cast something that made her move faster and muted her steps. The lack of audio and visual cues was disorienting and almost nauseating. She had to think of something else to stay balanced. "I don't understand something," she said to Pester. "Why are the imps going so calmly together to the marsh? Why aren't they attacking each other?"

"They're following rules set down by Lord Accuse. The rules of battle for a drudge are as follows," Pester began. "One: For the full life of each drudge, only one challenger may attempt to steal them. Two: When a challenger steps forward, the owner of the drudge is obliged to defend their property on the Battle Marsh. Three: As you learned last night, the fight is to the death. Four: No matter who wins the battle, the drudge—as I said—may not be stolen again. Five: The victor gets full rights against any and all other claimants."

"So, whoever wins today—" began Nia.

"—gets to keep Tanni until he dies," Pester said in conclusion.

Nia shuddered. The spells were working. She was only fifty yards away, and there was no sign the imps noticed they were being followed. Suddenly, her throat tightened, and she asked, "Since Tanni's been stolen once, doesn't that mean I can't steal him?"

"You're not an imp," Pester replied in amusement.

They were getting closer still when Ease whispered, "Hold back a bit. I know you want your friend but wait till the battle begins."

Nia backed off, leaving seventy yards of distance between the opponents and herself. Looking the two imps over, her blood ran cold. No beauty was left in their demon-like features. Their skin was dark gray, almost charred in appearance, their noses nearly flat on their deeply wrinkled faces. As the two traded insults, she realized the one on the right, the slightly uglier of the two, was Vex.

"How dare you challenge me, an Original!" Vex thundered, his voice echoing unnaturally over the flat, boggy expanse.

"You're not an Original, dimwit. No Original pays lip service to an underling. I saw you back at the clearing," sneered his opponent. "The small imp was ordering you around, and you obeyed him!"

"I obey no underling. Grovel on the ground and repent," Vex commanded, "or face my wrath, crook!"

"Never!"

"Then prepare to die," Vex sneered.

The two imps charged each other, firing and dodging spells. Nia stood transfixed by their fury, overtaken with fascination and wonder. Then, Wither hissed in her ear to get moving. On her right shoulder, Pester was panting. On her left, Ease held fast to her hair. Moving stealthily forward, Nia ignored the shouts, flashes, and clashes from the battle and prepared to grab Tanni.

Unseen by any, she'd just reached out and grabbed Tanni's arm when a loud shriek echoed through the air. Looking up, Nia saw Vex latched onto his opponent midflight. A dim light shone in his core.

"No!" screamed the other imp. "It can't be!"

"Oh, it can. As I told you," Vex gloried, "I knew once what it was to shine!" A brilliant flash erupted from his body. His opponent let out a final shriek and vanished. Dust floated harmlessly away in the morning breeze.

Nia looked back at Tanni, but he was gone! Or was he? She couldn't see him, but she felt his arm in her grasp. To her amazement, she realized Ease must have concealed him while she was distracted. Heart pounding, Nia pulled at the boy. She felt him turn and come with her. Encouraged, she hurried Tanni away from the marsh, while Vex crowed in triumph in the sky. She quickly made it halfway to the tree line, listening to Wither, who quietly coached her forward.

Suddenly, a startled scream rang against the near trees. Nia felt eyes bore into the back of her head. Then, with a blast wave that tore across the open marsh, the concealment that covered all of them shattered. Tanni came abruptly into view. Panic surged through Nia as her own hand became visible, and she suddenly saw Wither hovering next to her head.

"You!" Vex roared.

Nia pivoted as he barreled through the air toward her. His palm flashed, and she dove to the ground, pulling Tanni down with her. Vex's spell whizzed just above her head and exploded in the nearby mud.

Wither let out a terrified shriek and fled toward the forest. Pester and Ease got off the ground where Nia's fall had thrown them. Taking to the air around Nia and Tanni, they cast shielding spells to protect them.

"Vex, halt! I order you to halt!" Pester shouted.

Vex laughed darkly. Shaking his head, he said, "You know, Pester, for some reason your commands have no effect on me anymore. I don't know what happened, little starfly, but it's as if you died. You realize dead masters have no control over their servants, don't you?"

Pester let out a frightened squeak. Vex's eyes darted to Ease.

"Oh, Ease," he sneered, "I'm disappointed in you. Surely you had better tactics for recapturing your Starbeam than this. I'll enjoy killing you all before dragging the boy back to the mines."

Vex dove toward the two sprites. Nia watched in horror but was blinded by a brilliant flash of light exploding simultaneously from Ease and Pester. Blinking to clear her vision, she noticed the clash had knocked Vex and the sprites several yards from each other. Stunned by the flash, each stumbled to find their footing. Taking advantage of the lull in fighting, Nia reached for Tanni to pull him back to his feet. Immediately, she felt Vex's eyes upon her. Glancing back, she saw malicious intent flood his features.

"Very well," he said darkly, swooping at her. "You die first!"

Terrified, Nia leapt out of his way, tripping in the process. Falling prone on her stomach, she heard Vex swoop back toward her. Cowering and covering her neck with her arms, the wind of his wings beat down on her back. Then, a bright form came at him sideways, knocking the oversized imp into a pool of water.

Nia looked up just in time to see Vex resurface and shoot a spell at Ease, who crashed instantly to the ground. Nia choked back a startled cry.

Crowing in delight, Vex climbed out of the pool and headed back toward Nia. She scrambled away, but he was too fast. Hovering above her, he raised a hand and prepared a spell for the killing blow. "Good-bye," he said with a sneer.

Before Vex had finished speaking the word, a brilliant flash struck his left side, sending him barreling into the mud. Pester swooped in for another attack, but Nia waved him off. Surprised, Pester landed next to Ease.

Vex's ribs were crushed in on one side. Gasping for air, blood came out of his mouth. Nia stared into his dark eyes, and her heart sank. Nothing good remained within him. Pity filled her heart.

"I'll kill you for this," Vex coughed, opening a palm toward her.

Nia didn't give him time to cast his spell. Lifting her foot over him, she closed her eyes and stepped down on his head. A horrible crunching sound filled the air.

CHAPTER 27

Sickened by the drastic turn of events, Nia shielded her eyes from the crushed imp. It horrified and nauseated her to think she'd just killed him. Stepping away, she hurriedly rinsed her foot in the oily pool near Vex's body, then crouched next to Pester. He was cradling Ease's head with a pained expression. Ease's eyes were closed, her light very dim. "Is she dead?" Nia asked, her voice trembling.

"No. But she's near death. My mother found me in this state once, as you may recall. The spell she used to revive me burned my skin for days. At the time, I could have almost traced it, if I'd dared. I might still be able to remember its pattern now, but I need quiet to concentrate," Pester shuddered. Pointing at a nearby tree, he said, "I'll be up there. I won't be far. In the meantime, Nia, hold onto Ease. She needs you."

"Needs me?" Nia breathed incredulously. "No one needs me."

"We all need you," said Pester, catching her eye. Without another word, he flew off.

Picking up Ease's limp body, Nia cradled her like an infant. "Don't leave me, Ease," she begged the unconscious sprite. "Don't prove what I already believe to be the real truth about myself.

Don't show me what I already know. I know I'm not wanted. I know I kill everything I touch. Why show me this when we were so close to getting home? Why didn't you sacrifice me instead of yourself? We'd all have been better off for it, don't you see?"

"None of us would have been better off for it."

The voice made Nia jump. She turned her head and saw Tanni crouching next to her. His grime-caked face was gaunt, his eyes dark and haunting. Still, he held her gaze and wanly smiled, "You were, after all, the guiding light for us all."

Tears started in Nia's eyes. "How can you say that?" she choked. "Tanni, look at yourself. Look at Ease!"

"I can't see her, Nia. I can't," said Tanni heavily. "But what I can see is your glow."

Nia looked at her hands and shook her head. "That's the sprite's light," she said dully. "I contain none myself."

"No, Nia. You've been getting it all wrong. That's your light reflecting off of Ease. Your light shines. Sprites are but moons mirroring back what they receive."

Could it be true? Do I really hold light within myself? Nia thought doubtfully. Then, she saw Tanni lower his head and begin to cry. "Tanni," she asked, "what's wrong?"

The weary boy only shook his head. But Nia kept prompting. Finally, he cried, "Where'd my light go, Nia? Where'd it go? You know where I think it went? I squandered it. I ignored The Lumen and rushed headlong into danger. I thought I was invincible. But I wasn't. I thought I was smarter than him. I was wrong. It's my fault. It's all my fault."

Shifting Ease to her right arm, Nia placed her free hand on Tanni's shoulder. "You did what you thought was right. I don't blame you," she said gently. "Who could?"

"I could. The Lumen could. How can I go home to face him now? How can I even look him in the eye after I've proven just how selfish and self-serving I am? I wanted to be praised, Nia. I wanted glory. That's why I apprenticed myself to the Lightkeepers. But I failed! And you know what? That's what I am, just a big, stupid failure." Tanni buried his face in his hands. His shoulders shook as he spoke. "No one needs me. I doubt anyone wants me."

"Tanni," pleaded Nia, "you followed your heart here. I wouldn't be the same if you hadn't come. I'd be a lifeless shell."

"But look at me!" Tanni wept, gesturing at himself wildly. "Look at how dark I've become. This is all I deserve now. This is all I am, don't you see?"

"What happened to you does not define you!" cried Nia, suddenly realizing her statement was just as relevant to herself as to him. Stunned, she sat there, momentarily unable to speak. Finding her voice again at last, she stammered, "I ran off into the woods after my Nanna yelled at me. I lost my light too. Does that define who and what I am?"

Tanni's eyes widened. Slowly he shook his head and said quietly, "I've never thought so. I see the point you're making. You're absolutely right. But you know, speaking of that, I've thought a lot about your story. Do you really think you ran off just because your Nanna lost her patience?"

"What do you mean?" asked Nia, confused.

"Where did your fear of being a burden really come from? Did you already have it when you left for your Nanna's house?"

Nia grew quiet and reflective. Straining her brain, she could just make out the memory of feeling unwanted even in her own house. But she couldn't quite figure out why. All at once, it came to her. Drawing in a shuddering breath, she said shakily, "I had it at home too. My mother's belly was growing bigger and bigger. She kept telling me I'd have a new brother or sister soon. My whole world started to upend. They moved me out of their bedroom, saying they needed space for the cradle. Mom had no energy to play with me. Dad became busier and more distant. By the time Nanna came to pick me up, I was convinced that my parents didn't want me anymore and were sending me off for good. I guess in a way, they were. They just didn't know it yet."

"So, after reflecting on this," Tanni began gently, "do you still think you're a burden?"

Nia glanced down at Ease. The sprite looked so peaceful. She wondered if that was how it would be when she was near death. "I don't know," she admitted.

Suddenly, Tanni reached out and lifted her chin. Nia's heart skipped. Looking up at him, she saw kindness reflected in his eyes.

Swallowing to clear his throat, Tanni said firmly, "Nia, let me remind you how sad your family has been without you in their circle. They've kept your room exactly how it was when you left it. They celebrate your birthday every year, even inviting family and friends over to grieve your absence. They lay a wreath for you on their remembrance stone and keep your favorite flowers planted there. They've taught your sister, Rosa, your favorite tunes. The walls of your parents' bedroom include drawings of your face. They light candles beneath them and pray to the stars that you'll come home. The walls of your Nanna's home are covered with artwork you once drew for her. Let me say this loud and clear: You are wanted."

The words reverberated through Nia. Pulling away from Tanni, she covered her face with her free hand as bittersweet tears poured from her eyes. Allowing his last phrase to wash over her, it slowly cleansed and liberated her from the lies she'd told herself for so many years. It was as if a spell had broken.

"All these years since you got to the Shadelands you've been projecting your belief of being unwanted onto every person you've ever met. But you know what?" Tanni said softly. "It's time to let that go. It's time to be free."

Looking up at him through her tears, Nia smiled, "It's time you were free too, Tanni. You are not a failure."

"Thank you," Tanni smiled. "You are not a burden."

As the two gazed at one another, Pester landed at Nia's side. His form was brighter than it had been a few minutes before, but his brow was creased in concentration.

"You've done an amazing job of keeping Ease alive with your light, Nia. But now I need you to set her down. Once you do," he said nervously, "both of you stand back. If I get this wrong, who knows what kind of calamity might come upon us."

Tanni started. Nia turned and saw that his eyes were wide, his face pale. "Who spoke with you just now?" he asked frantically. "Was that your imp?"

"Yes, that was Pester," Nia admitted, wiping away her tears. "But he's not an imp anymore. He's a sprite. I can explain later."

Tanni scratched his head in bewilderment. Nia looked from him to Pester, who continued to stare intently at the sprite in her arms. Gently she placed Ease on the ground and said, "Here she is. Did you remember your mother's rune?"

"I think so," Pester replied. "I hope so. Back up now. Pray I don't make a mistake and kill myself and Ease in the process—or you both will be in a world of trouble."

Tanni and Nia backed away several feet, Tanni still visibly shaken. As Nia held her breath, Pester lifted Ease's hand and drew something on it. Nothing happened. Knitting his brows together tighter, Pester closed his eyes in thought. Nia took a few shallow breaths, praying to nothing in particular that this might work.

Suddenly, a grin spread across Pester's face. "I think have it!"

Moving to Ease's forehead, Pester tried the rune again. A brilliant flash of light exploded out of him. Ease stirred and her eyes fluttered. Panting, Pester collapsed next to her. "It worked," he said between breaths. "It worked, and I'm not dust."

Several seconds passed before Ease opened her eyes and sat up. The first thing her eyes fell upon was Vex's crushed form. Her peaceful expression shifted instantly to grief and horror. "So passes Soothe," she said grimly. "May his light pass to another."

"Look, Ease," Pester said with tired excitement, "you're alive, and I didn't blow us up!"

Ease smiled at Peter's enthusiasm and said in amazement, "Pester, you are more than meets the eye."

"I think that's been true since the day you first met me," Pester chuckled.

Happy over Ease's restoration, Nia was just about to suggest the group get ready to go, when Tanni swooned against her. Attempting to hold him up, she got knocked down under him instead. The two hit the ground hard, and Nia got the wind knocked out of her when his body landed across her back. Sprawled on the muddy ground beneath him and wheezing to catch her breath, she called for help. The two sprites swiftly landed next to her head. But before they could do anything, Tanni came to with a moan and rolled off her without any help.

Ease scanned the area anxiously. "We've been in the open too long," she said. "Let's get him to the cave. I'll restore him there. Then, Pester and I will cast wingfoot on the two of you, and we'll head off to Portal Hill."

"Portal Hill?" panted Nia, helping Tanni get dizzily to his feet.

"The hill where the Lightkeepers' camp was," Ease explained. "I made a deal with The Lumen that I'd alert him when I was ready to come home so he could open a portal for me and any other travelers with me. I can't do that until we are closer to the hill."

Nia turned to Tanni, who hadn't heard his sprite, and explained Ease's plan. He nodded weakly. With Tanni draped over her shoulder, Nia walked to the cave where she'd spent the night. After Ease restored Tanni, and he and Nia had eaten, Tanni was at last ready to go. Nia smiled to see him glowing again, if only faintly. Tanni slung his pack and Nia followed him out of the cave. Once outside, wingfoot was cast on both of them. Ease took Tanni's shoulder and Pester climbed on Nia's. Then, the two children shot off, relieved to finally be headed home.

CHAPTER 28

It was late afternoon when the group reached the base of Portal Hill. It had been a relatively cheerful run for Nia. Tanni had talked more about his family and about Nia's sister, Rosa. Nia learned that Rosa liked many of the things she had liked as a child—playing with dolls, drawing flowers, and gathering interesting rocks. The more she heard, the more Nia longed to meet her. Now, seeing the hill where in just a few minutes she finally would, excitement rose in her throat.

"Have you contacted The Lumen yet?" she asked Ease.

"No—not yet," Ease said. She sounded puzzled and slightly alarmed. "Hold up a bit."

Nia pulled Tanni to a halt alongside her. "What is it?" he asked.

"Ease," Nia said to the sprite on Tanni's shoulder, "what's wrong? The last time I heard you talk like that it was just before Tanni was recaptured. What are you sensing?"

Just then, Pester gasped and stiffened against Nia's neck.

"Oh no," cried Ease. "We're not safe here. Run!"

Terror surged through Nia. Relaying Ease's command, she and Tanni bolted from the hill. But after only a few steps, Nia's legs froze up. She lunged forward onto the forest floor. The impact rattled her teeth and jarred her skull. Tanni flew into the dirt beside her. Several feet ahead, Ease and Pester rolled along the ground. The air become deadly cold.

"So, Vex's murderers have come to call, have they?" laughed Lord Accuse, appearing in front of the children. "This ought to be interesting." With a wave of his palm, first Ease and then Pester were drawn through the air and dumped next to Tanni.

Nia watched Lord Accuse raise his hand at her next. Her body responded automatically, and she was made to sit up. Tanni was left where he was.

Lord Accuse stood a head taller than Vex. His features weren't entirely hideous, but they were dark and twisted by malice. His face was careworn, its expression icy. Teeth chattering, Nia sought any light within the imp lord. She saw nothing. Whatever light he once had was buried and hidden. Cunning filled his eyes, eyes that glared into her own. She squirmed. It was as if he was looking into her soul.

"Selfish girl," he began softly. "You made your Nanna cry. You wrecked her health and her whole life. You wrecked the lives of all your family. Happy about that, unwanted little burden?"

Nia sucked in a breath, feeling as if her heart had been stabbed. What he said felt so justified. Yes, her poor Nanna. Her poor parents. It was all her fault. She'd caused all of it. Stinging tears started in her eyes. Lord Accuse chuckled darkly and moved on to Tanni.

"You're an incompetent failure, did you know that? You couldn't even execute your plan correctly. Now, The Lumen wants nothing more to do with you. Your very name brings shame to the Lightkeepers. You're the example The Lumen uses to stop other fools from attempting the suicide mission you went on." As Lord Accuse spoke, Tanni hid his face in the dirt. Soon, the sound of sobbing poured out of him.

Moving on to Pester, Lord Accuse laughed, "Oh yes, the little vermin I once offered a job to. You never were anything to me. I saw your past the moment I first laid eyes on you. You are so pathetic you couldn't even control the mind of a helpless five-year-old girl. And now, your name will become a byword across the entire Shadelands. We'll call anything a Pester that's so weak and utterly pitiful that the only thing to do is put it out of its misery." Pester squeaked. His head dropped in shame.

Lord Accuse grinned and moved on to Ease. "Oh yes, the dimmest glowing sprite in the Sunlands. You win first place when it comes to losing Starbeams to my realm. That's got to sting a bit, no? Still, I've got to thank you for your generous donations. You stood by and watched those Starbeams go one by one, never trying to stop them. Only when Tanni went through did you finally go too. Guess his grandmother, Ira, wasn't worth the trouble, huh?"

Ease opened her mouth, but then closed it. She had nothing to say in response.

"Well, after that very touching tell-all, how about we get to the good news," began Lord Accuse. "None of you will be leaving this spot alive. I thought of killing the sprites first, but now I've decided against it. It'll be much more moving to have Ease and Pester watch their drudges slowly die. I'll start with Nia."

At his words, Nia's blood ran cold. She'd gotten so close to leaving, but now, this was it. She would never get to apologize to her family for the trouble she put them through. She would die an unwanted burden, just as Lord Accuse had said.

As Lord Accuse came up behind her and wrapped a freezing cold, taloned hand around her throat, Nia looked ahead hopelessly, only to catch a glimpse of Wither peeking at her from behind a tree. In Wither's hand was a pinecone. Nia stared at it for half a second in confusion, before the meaning of it dawned on her. Courage seeped back through her, and she said boldly, "I'm not an unwanted burden, you know."

Lord Accuse hissed and released her throat. Walking in front of her, he looked her square in the face. "What was that?" he demanded, his icy glare boring into her.

"I'm not an unwanted burden," she said calmly. "Those who love me most would agree." To her surprise, she felt and saw her hands light up in her lap. She hadn't even realized she'd stopped shining.

"What, you mean the ones you've led blindly into a trap?" Lord Accuse sneered, rubbing his chin. "The ones you've just betrayed?"

"You're the betrayer, Truth!" Nia said, her eyes flashing. "You betrayed the entire race of sprites in your pointless little rebellion. Because of it, no one loves you. I'm sure that hurts a bit, doesn't it?"

Lord Accuse back handed her, and she landed painfully on her side, her ears ringing. As she lay momentarily stunned, something came between her and the imp lord. A spell from Lord Accuse fizzled out right in front of her eyes.

"Impossible!" he breathed in fury.

A strange peace washed over Nia. *Truth comes to those who look for it*, said a voice which echoed in her mind. At first, she was confused. The only sprite she'd known to go by that name had been Lord Accuse himself. But then, she thought she understood. Somehow, by increasing her light in Lord Accuse's presence, she'd awakened the truth that was hidden within him, and now Truth was standing invisibly between her and his twisted, deadly form.

The invisible something touched Nia's head and understanding was infused into her mind. Everything Lord Accuse was hiding was laid bare before her. Filled with wonder, light flared up within her and the holding spell broke. Cursing under his breath, Lord Accuse stepped in front of her, another spell sparkling in his hand. At this, adrenaline surged through Nia. Without thinking, she grabbed his wrists and forced him to shoot the spell into the canopy. Ease, Pester, and Tanni gasped in surprise.

Lord Accuse squirmed in Nia's grasp. His icy skin froze her to the core, but her hands felt like they were on fire. In spite of this, she remained calm. Looking into his cold, black gaze, she said quietly, "You've lost the power to hide the truth, Truth. I know your past. I know your pain. You've spent all this time tortured by frustration and rage. You entered the Realm Beyond with the firm belief that your glow, unhindered by Starbeams, would grow brighter than the sun. Instead, you found only darkness and despair."

"Let me go!" Lord Accuse demanded, kicking and spitting in Nia's face. But his strength was like that of a tiny child's. Even with her hands going numb, Nia managed to hold on.

"You spent your days firm in the belief that you were the most intelligent and cunning of all creatures that ever lived," Nia continued fiercely. "But there's one thing you refused to know. You refused to discover where a sprite's light truly originates— Starbeam joy. You are but a mirror of my light. You feed off this light and shine it back to further increase my happiness. But the system you've been using is unsustainable. Your light is almost gone. Someday it'll burn out altogether. You've neared the end. The clock is ticking."

"Liar! Useless, pitiful, worthless child! You bring harm to everyone you see! Must you burden the entire world?"

"The past you're using to shame me holds no power over me anymore," said Nia, her light growing brighter by the moment. "I've died to it and new seeds have grown. You're too late. You can't trap me anymore with your lies. They've been exposed for what they really are. I've come back to the light where no darkness can reach me. I am already free!"

At the word free, Nia's skin blazed forth with sudden and unequaled fury, sending a scorching jet of light straight from her heart through Lord Accuse's chest. The light blasted him from her hands into a nearby tree. The sound of thunder reverberated across the sky. To Nia's astonishment, shadows fled as trees and dirt began to glow. The ground beneath her feet trembled. Nia saw the bonds on Pester, Ease, and Tanni break just as Wither wailed and threw herself onto the shining forest floor. Then, all around Nia portals started opening.

Drawn to the portal nearest her, Nia started walking toward it, but she felt something latch onto her ankle. Looking down startled, she saw Lord Accuse feebly holding onto her, his chest singed and smoking. "Save me," he whimpered piteously.

At that moment, a tall, brilliantly glowing man stepped through the portal in front of her, the emblem of a pinecone embroidered on his tunic. The radiance of his form was so great Nia could barely look at him. At her feet, Lord Accuse yelped.

"Nia, I presume?" the man asked. Nia nodded as several more Starbeams walked through behind him.

"Well done, Nia. Well done." The stranger sounded amazed and proud. "And Tanni," he said, looking past Nia, "thank you for ignoring my command. The Realm Beyond is only free because of you."

"You're The Lumen?" asked Nia. The stranger didn't answer, but responded only with a knowing, gracious smile. Glancing down at Accuse, she said, "The lord of this realm just asked me to save him. What should I do?"

Peering with eyes like the sun at the imp lord, The Lumen said firmly, "It's over, Truth. Release your hold on this realm so it can be restored. If you refuse, you and all the imps beneath you will come to a swift and terrible end."

Grimly, Lord Accuse nodded. With a blast of his hand, the remaining darkness was dispersed, and light flooded the canopy. At this, the portals converged and the Sunlands appeared to merge with the Shadelands. Beautiful fields of wildflowers, small cottages, gardens, and grain fields came into view behind Portal hill. Nia heard Wither sobbing nearby. Looking back, she saw

Pester comforting her. Then, as if a switch had gone off, hundreds of sprites began pouring into the Shadelands.

"The age of imps is over," The Lumen said. "The land belongs to sprites now. I leave it to them to judge what to do with their impish kin. Nia, Tanni," he continued, turning to the children, "it's time you came home."

CHAPTER 29

Nia smiled at the new lullaby Pester sang softly into her ear. The words were hopeful and full of new purpose. She had every reason to feel that hope. She was in the Sunlands where she belonged. Walking on the outskirts of Thistlespray with Tanni and The Lumen, she clutched a bouquet of flowers. All around her, the air was sweetly scented with wildflowers. The breeze was soft and warm, the sky a brilliant blue. Taking it all in, Nia shivered with wonder and excitement. Sitting on Tanni's shoulder, Ease smiled and hummed along with Pester's song.

It was morning. The Lumen had arranged for the children to spend the night in the camp on Portal Hill. While they slept, messengers were sent ahead to their families, informing them of their children's homecoming. Before departing the camp, the children had bathed and received fresh tunics and pants. Nia's hair had been trimmed to remove years of mats. Even though she'd overcome many worries, she was comforted to know that her family's first view of her wouldn't be of a filthy, flea-bitten girl in rags.

Before she'd left, she ensured Wither would be well taken care of. The Lightkeepers had agreed to take her on as their Shadelands guide while they searched for lost Starbeams. To Nia's relief, they treated Wither kindly. At their parting, Nia promised her to visit often. Wither thanked her for shaking things up a bit, but then joked that—perhaps, she had shaken them up a little too much.

"Nia, slow down a bit, will you?" Wither laughed. "Keep going at this rate and you could bring about the end of the world!"

At a bend in the hill, Nia's heart leapt into her throat. Thistlespray village had just come into view and ahead of her were at least a hundred glowing people waiting to see her and Tanni. Among them were two families out front, one of which included her parents, nanna, and a young girl Nia could only assume was Rosa.

Feeling her legs nearly give way beneath her, Nia urgently whispered to The Lumen, "Don't tell them what I did in the Shadelands. I don't want them to think of me as a hero."

The Lumen and Tanni stared at her in surprise. The sprites were taken aback. "Why shouldn't I share?" asked The Lumen. "You are a hero, Nia."

"I only protected myself and those I loved," said Nia, looking at the ground. "That's nothing to be remembered for."

The Lumen patted her head. "If you wish it," he laughed. "I'll keep it to myself for now. But, my dear, whether you accept it or not, you'll be remembered long after you have passed, specifically because you protected those you loved. Come, your family is waiting."

The last paces that separated Nia from her family felt simultaneously like too many and too few. Before she knew it, she'd reached them. Tanni's family wasted no time rushing forward to embrace him. His brother, Fiddi, socked him in the shoulder and mockingly demanded where he'd been.

Nia took in the hungry expressions of her own family. Walking timidly to her nanna, she gave her half the flowers. Her nanna looked grief stricken, and uttered Nia a quiet apology. Nia shook her head and cried, "Nanna, you couldn't have stopped what happened. It was me who chose to run. I'm so sorry!"

At this, Nanna and Nia's parents rushed to embrace her. Pester took to the air to avoid being crushed by the sobbing Starbeams. It seemed an hour before they let her go. When they finally did, Nia noticed the entire village watching her. Not a dry eye was in sight.

Seeing her sister standing to the side and looking forlorn, Nia bent down to her and said softly, "Hi, Rosa. I'm sorry I robbed you of an older sister. I want to fix that. Let's be friends." Smiling at her hopefully, she saw Rosa smile shyly back.

It was a day unlike any other. Villagers hugged Nia, a party was thrown for her, she ate strange and colorful foods that brought happy tears to her eyes, and she played games with Rosa to both their hearts' content.

In a brief pause from the festivities, Pester came to land on Nia's shoulder, his eyes brimming with pleasure.

"Ease has given me a new name," he said proudly, pushing his chest out. "She's called me Reflect."

"Why Reflect?" Nia asked, puzzled.

"Because, for one, I reflect you. Whether you're happy or sad, I'll be able to see it. On top of that, I have a past unlike any other. I'll be reflecting on that past for a lifetime," said Pester, smiling thoughtfully.

Nia grinned at the pleased sprite. "It's perfect," she said. "I couldn't think of a better or more fitting name."

"Neither could I," Pester sighed in contentment.

The two looked at each other, and in that moment, Nia knew the Sunlands couldn't have been complete without him.

EPILOGUE

In the darkness of a cozy room, a sprite sat on a bookshelf across from where Nia lay tranquilly sleeping in her soft bed. Peacefully he watched over her, pondering the strange turn his life had taken. His name was Reflect, and he was very happy.

ABOUT THE AUTHOR

As a young woman, Rachel Randall spent time in Latvia, a beautiful eastern European country along the Baltic Sea, immersing herself in the local language and culture. Aspects of their folklore—the Daughters of the Sun, and devils who kidnap people and drag them through forest entrances to their world—were used in the creation of Shadelands, her first book. Currently, Randall lives on a wooded hill near Seattle with her husband and two children.